I0679259

Sherlock Holmes and

The Adventure Of

The Black Pharaoh

By

JM Reinbold

Hardcover ISBN 978-1-80424-628-3
Paperback ISBN 978-1-80424-629-0
ePub ISBN 978-1-80424-630-6
PDF ISBN 978-1-80424-631-3

MX Publishing, 335 Princess Park Manor, Royal Drive,
London, N11 3GX
www.mxpublishing.com

Cover design by Awan

In Memory of

Ramona DeFelice Long

Chapter One

We were a fortnight into December of 1890. The weather, increasingly cold, turned bitter overnight. I awoke to a howling wind flinging icy pellets against the rattling windowpanes, and a profound ache in my leg, the result of a wound I suffered during the Second Anglo-Afghan war. After partaking of one of Mrs. Hudson's bracing winter breakfasts, I put my feet up on the fender hoping to pass a restorative morning reading by the fire.

"Have you seen this, Holmes?" I exclaimed, holding up *The Times*. "Sir Roger Trumbull has been murdered. His hands were cut off and carried away by the killer!"

"A member of the Henry expedition, I believe," Holmes replied.

"What?"

"Sir Roger was an Egyptologist with the British Museum was he not?"

"Oh, yes. Quite right."

The mysteries of ancient Egypt, a topic of conversation from the meanest hovels of the working class to the grandest drawing rooms of the elite, enthralled the public. Even Holmes was not immune.

My friend rubbed his hands together, his eyes gleaming with expectation. "Mayhap, Watson, Sir Roger's death will bring some work my way and dispel this boredom that afflicts me. It is just the type of affair that utterly confounds the police."

"The vulgar press is connecting it to Lord Convarran's disappearance and putting it down to a pharaoh's curse."

"Of course, they are, Watson. That is what the indiscriminate public craves."

"Well, you know, Holmes …"

"Kindly refrain from defending them, Watson." He fixed me with his steely grey eyes. "It is the sort of device you employ in your little stories of my deductions, playing upon the appeal of the fantastic rather than the facts."

"Really, Holmes, your critique is unfair!"

"Humph!" He raised his newspaper and would say no more.

As the day wore on, Holmes shuttled between his desk and his chemistry table, clipping crime reports, perusing his correspondence, dispatching replies, and puttering about with his experiments. Periodically, he went to the window and gazed down into the street.

"Surely, Holmes, you're not expecting a client in this weather?"

"On the contrary, Watson, their coach approaches as we speak."

My curiosity getting the better of me, I bestirred myself and joined him at the window. A private coach, a heraldic seal emblazoned on its side, pulled by four black horses, slid to a stop in the snow-filled street. A liveried coachman jumped down and crossed the pavement to our door. The bell clanged followed by the quick tread of Billy, our pageboy, hurrying to answer the summons, with Mrs. Hudson's slower step coming along after him. Within seconds came a clatter on the stairs. Holmes, already at our door, opened it to a beaming Billy who, pulling himself up to his full height, thrust a silver salver at him with a calling card upon it.

"A lord and lady to see you, Mr. Holmes!" he cried.

Holmes glanced at the card. A smile flickered upon his lips. "Pray show our distinguished visitors the way up."

"Straight away, Mr. Holmes!" said the lad and was off again like a shot.

I turned back to the window. The driver let down the coach's step and opened the door for his passengers. A man emerged, and then turned to help a woman. I could tell they were young – I reckoned not more than twenty years of age. Both were dressed from head to toe in black. When the lady had gained her footing in the icy track, the two men took up positions on either side of her and so they made their way into the house. We soon heard footsteps ascending the stairs and Billy reappeared to announce our guests.

"Lord Silverpin and the Honorable Vivienne Henry," he said. With a flourish, he ushered them inside.

Lord Silverpin and Lady Vivienne were quite striking. They wore long coats and kubankas, Russian-style hats of Astrakhan fur. Their kid gloves were trimmed with the same fur, and both carried ebony walking sticks topped with gold.

"Lord Silverpin, Lady Vivienne, come, warm yourselves by the fire," said Holmes.

Our guests removed their coats and hats and, along with their sticks, handed them off to Mrs. Hudson who hung them on the coat stand beside our door.

Lord Silverpin addressed Holmes. "The weather is fierce, and we do not wish to keep our man waiting. However, our narrative will take some time to relate. Would you be so kind as to provide our coachman with a hot beverage?"

"Mrs. Hudson!" Holmes cried.

"Certainly, your Lordship, he shall have it right away," she replied.

While this exchange transpired, Billy stood, mouth agape, goggling at our visitors. I can't say I blamed him for a handsomer couple I have never seen. The young lord was tall, but not exceptionally so. His raven hair, grown long, was tied at the back with a ribbon. His features were delicate yet regal, as were Lady Vivienne's. And she, the most perfect specimen of femininity I have ever encountered. From her intricately piled tresses, as black as his and pricked with jewels, to her dainty booted feet, she exuded a heady demeanor that captivated my every sense. Yet, it was their eyes that struck me most, green as emeralds, intelligent, and probing. Lady Vivienne extended her tiny, gloved hand. Startled, as Holmes had yet to introduce us, I received her hand gently and kissed it, perhaps lingering a bit overlong, transfixed by an unusual, seductive scent that for a moment rendered me quite giddy.

Mrs. Hudson coughed, breaking my trance. As I relinquished the lady's hand and stepped back, our housekeeper curtsied, nudging Billy, who bobbed a bow. The two of them then hustled off to see about the coachman.

"Now then," said Holmes, eyeing me with what I perceived as mild amusement. "Allow me to introduce my friend and colleague, Dr. Watson. You may speak freely in his presence."

After formally acknowledging our guests, I fetched two more chairs and placed them near the fire.

"May I offer you a sherry?" Holmes inquired.

"That would be most welcome," said Lady Vivienne. "We are chilled to the bone."

"You are fraternal twins, are you not?" Holmes asked nonchalantly as he poured four glasses of our best sherry. "In fact, you've devoted some effort to accentuating your similarities."

Lord Silverpin's eyes narrowed as he gave Holmes a shrewd look. "Indeed, you are correct, Mr. Holmes."

"I beg your pardon; I meant no offense. It is interesting though, that rather than seek differentiation, you seek a greater resemblance to one another."

"We have always felt as though we were one person divided into two," Lady Vivienne said.

"Of course," murmured Holmes. "The sensation of separation where it is perceived there should be none. Fascinating."

Fearing Holmes's insatiable curiosity had intruded on too private a matter, I suggested we take our seats. After we had settled by the fire, I endeavored to engage our guests in a bit of light conversation.

Holmes, undeterred by his social gaffe, interrupted my postulations about the weather to inquire, "How may I serve you, your Lordship?"

"Your pardon, Dr. Watson," Lord Silverpin said as he turned away from me and addressed my friend. "Our father, Robert Henry, the fifth Earl of Convarran, has been missing for more than two months and as yet no trace of him has been found. The police are baffled, and we are at our wits' end."

"I have no doubt of that," Holmes replied. "I have followed the story in the papers with some interest. I take it there has been no communication, no ransom demand, no ultimatum, no other requests?"

"None," said Lady Vivienne.

"Pray, tell me, what were the circumstances of your father's disappearance? Include all the details, even those that seem of no consequence. Leave nothing out."

Holmes leaned back in his chair, closed his eyes, and rested his hands upon his breast as if in contemplation.

Our guests looked to me. "His posture is Holmes's way of focusing on your every word," I reassured them.

"Just so," said he. "Pray begin."

"Very well," said Lord Silverpin. "As you may also know from the papers, our father is an amateur archaeologist with a keen interest in Egyptology. His last expedition was to Dahshoor where he and three associates, Sir Roger Trumbull, Professor J. Ambrose Emm, and the great adventurer, Mr. Cedric Matheson, conducted excavations on the Black Pyramid and the surrounding necropolis. They stayed little more than a month before abandoning the site and returning home. Then on the thirteenth of October, our father retired to his study to complete preparations for an exhibition at the Egyptian Hall. We saw no more of him that evening. That is not unusual for he often works late into the night. The following day, he did not appear for breakfast. This also is not unusual. He often goes to his bed in the early hours of the morning, sometimes not at all, but naps upon the divan in his study."

At this point, Lady Vivienne took up the story.

"We were first concerned when he failed to appear by mid-morning to leave for London. I went to his bedchamber and found it unoccupied. I then went to his study. The door was locked, as is his habit when he does not wish to be disturbed, and though I knocked and called, he did not answer."

"We then consulted our butler and our housekeeper. Neither had received any communication from him. Father's valet told us he had not seen him since the evening before when he dressed him for dinner. The following morning, when he went to Father's bed chamber to prepare his *toilette*, he found the room empty and the bed unused."

Holmes looked up. "Did none of these servants go to your father's study to see if he required anything?"

"No, Mr. Holmes. Our father forbade the servants to enter his study or otherwise disturb him on pain of immediate dismissal."

"Has this always been so?" Holmes asked.

"No, he issued this directive after his return from Egypt."

Holmes nodded. "Go on," he said.

"Our coachman was to drive the exhibition crates to Whitchurch Station and supervise loading them onto our private train, then return for father and his valet, as they intended to accompany the crates to London. On arrival at Paddington, the crates would be sent on to the Egyptian Hall. Father would then go on to our house in Mayfair where he planned to stay until after the exhibition. Staunton confirmed he had transported the crates and father, but at a much earlier hour than scheduled. When questioned, he stated father wished to make an early start and because he would be in London only a short time, he did not require his valet. A footman at our Mayfair house would suffice for his few needs."

"Why did your coachman not inform you of this change in plans immediately?" Holmes asked.

"It did not occur to him," Lord Silverpin replied. "He assumed our father had already done so. We did not realize father was missing until the staff at Mayfair telegraphed to say he had not appeared on the appointed day. It was then we contacted the police."

"What of the crates?" asked Holmes. "Could the contents have been the object of thieves? As I'm sure you are aware, there is a brisk trade in antiquities here at home as well as in Egypt."

"The crates were delivered to the Egyptian Hall," said Lady Vivienne. "They contained a mummy and assorted funerary objects from the tombs of various nobles. They contained nothing from royal burials or of great monetary value. We provided the police with a list of the contents."

"Who delivered them?" asked Holmes.

"Presumably, a carter hired at Paddington."

Adjusting his position and crossing his long legs, Holmes asked, "What conclusion have the police drawn?"

"That is why we have come to you, Mr. Holmes. The police have it all wrong."

"Have they," said Holmes. "I shouldn't wonder. Pray, elucidate."

"At first, the police believed the culprits to be Egyptian radicals who wish to keep foreign fortune-hunters out of Egypt. There have been threats in the past. However, due to a lack of evidence, they began to believe a rumor started by a member of the Egypt Exploration Fund who insinuated that our father's disappearance was a deception and that he would reappear at the mummy unwrapping exhibition at the Egyptian Hall where he intended to attract investors for his next expedition."

"Good Lord!" I exclaimed. "Mummy unwrapping! Are you serious?"

"Quite serious, I'm afraid, Dr. Watson. Unfortunately, such events are still *en vogue*."

"I perceive," Holmes said, "that you do not approve of such entertainments."

"You are correct, Mr. Holmes. The tide is beginning to turn away from exploitation, but as with any great change, progress is painfully slow."

"Did your father appear?" Holmes asked.

"There was no performance, Mr. Holmes. We cancelled it immediately."

"I don't mean to be indelicate," said Holmes, "but I must ask: Is your father given to such machinations?"

With some reluctance, Lord Silverpin replied, "He has always had a penchant for the theatrical. Pharaoh's curses and other macabre goings-on when bandied about in the daily papers ensure a good turn out and promises of authentic artifacts for personal collections attract investors."

Holmes leaned back in his chair and steepled his fingers. "However, in this case, you do not believe your father concocted this ballyhoo?"

"We do not," said Lady Vivienne, her voice tremulous with emotion. "He enjoys costumes, drama, and illusions, but he would not condescend to such vulgar deception."

"What of the other members of the expedition? What light can they shed upon your father's disappearance?" asked Holmes.

"The police have not been able to speak with Professor Emm. His servants say he is away on business," said Lord Silverpin.

"What?" said Holmes rising from his chair. "All this time? Where has the man gone?"

"The servants claim they do not know."

Holmes retrieved the sherry from the sideboard and refilled our glasses before returning to his seat.

"What of Matheson?"

"Mr. Matheson did not return home with the expedition. He went on to India to join a hunting party. He remained there and has only just heard of our father's disappearance. He is now *en route* to England."

"And poor Sir Roger," said Lady Vivienne, "In the past, he and the museum had been the recipient of threats from radicals demanding the return of artifacts they claimed were stolen by excavators. And that is not all, Mr. Holmes. Perhaps you saw in today's papers, Sir Roger was killed in a most grotesque way."

A tremor shook her whole body. Lord Silverpin placed a comforting hand on her arm.

"Yes," said Holmes. "And you fear a similar fate may have befallen your father."

"We do, Mr. Holmes. After our father's disappearance, we found an unusual scarab on the floor in his study. We did not associate it with his disappearance at the time. However, Inspector Lestrade discovered a scarab of the same kind on Sir Roger's body."

Holmes leaned forward in his chair. "Where are these scarabs now?"

"With the police," said Lord Silverpin.

"Scotland Yard has certainly made a hash of it," Holmes muttered. "Tell me, are there other persons who bear animosity, personal or professional, toward your father?"

Lord Silverpin drew in a long breath. "There are fierce rivalries for the best concessions and investors to be sure, but these men are gentlemen and scholars."

"Yet treasure is the object, is it not? Gentlemen and scholars they may be, but they all yearn for gold."

Lord Silverpin's cheeks flushed, and his lips settled into a hard line. "Of course, one dreams of discovering an undisturbed royal tomb with all its riches intact. What archaeologist does not?"

This time it was Lady Vivienne who placed a calming hand on her brother's arm.

"What can you tell me about your father's last expedition?" Holmes asked. "You said it ended prematurely. Why was that?"

"To be honest, we know surprisingly little about it," Lady Vivienne said. "Our father rarely spoke of it, and we did not press him as doing so caused him to become quite agitated. Perhaps there was a disagreement about methods or trouble with the hired workers or difficulties with the Service des Antiquities. Dahshoor is a sought-after concession, certainly not one to be abandoned without due course."

Holmes nodded. "You have given me little to start with, but I believe I may be able to penetrate the matter."

"You will help us then?" Lord Silverpin exclaimed.

A smile flickered across Holmes's lips. "Yes, your Lordship, I will endeavor to find your father. The situation has some intriguing features."

"Thank you, Mr. Holmes," said Lady Vivienne gracing my friend with a warm smile.

After bundling up against the cold once again, Lord Silverpin and Lady Vivienne bid us *adieu*. Holmes and I escorted our guests to the door.

"I would like to examine your father's study and your house and grounds," said Holmes.

Lord Silverpin gave Holmes a quizzical look. "But our father disappeared in London, Mr. Holmes. Will you not begin your search here?"

"His study is the last place your father was seen. I will begin my inquiries there," said Holmes.

"Very well," said Lord Silverpin. "We are returning to Highmount House today. Telegraph your schedule and we shall have a coach waiting for you."

"Excellent," said Holmes. "There is one other matter."

"Your fee, of course," said Lord Silverpin. "Be not concerned. Money is no object. Whatever the amount, it shall be paid."

"I have no doubt of it; that is not the matter. Rather, how it is that you came to consult me?"

"It was upon your brother's recommendation."

"Thank you," said Holmes. He bowed. "I bid you both good day. We shall call upon you on the morrow."

Chapter Two

The next morning, upon entering our sitting room, I found a blazing fire and Holmes, having already breakfasted, perusing *The Times*. I had barely started upon my own breakfast of savory eggs on toast before he threw down his paper and cried, "Come along, Watson. We've no time to lose."

"Whatever for?" I demanded. "Our train doesn't leave for hours."

"I must see Lestrade before we leave for Hampshire."

"Give me a moment, Holmes," I muttered.

"Do hurry, old man."

With mounting irritation, I stuffed my mouth with eggs and toast, washing it all down with gulps of coffee before scrambling to keep up with Holmes who had already adjusted his hat and was pulling on his gloves. I bundled into my overcoat and grabbed my hat and stick. Thus attired, we took up our traveling bags, and I my medical bag, and descended to the street. Despite Mrs. Hudson's strong coffee, I felt bleary-eyed and lethargic. A poor night's sleep plagued by dreams of which I had no memory had disquieted my mind. While Holmes hailed a cab, I collected a small picnic hamper from the larder, courtesy of our ever-thoughtful landlady. A few minutes later, I found a cab waiting at our door, with Holmes already inside.

In the early morning's stinging cold, the cabbie turned up his collar and huddled in his coat. He blew into his cupped, half-gloved hands while his horse puffed streams of steamy breath and stamped its hooves, impatient to be underway.

"Chop-chop, old man!" Holmes called cheerily as he flung open the door, "lest we freeze upon the spot!"

I sighed inwardly and clambered aboard, stowing the baggage on the seat beside me. I covered my legs with a lap rug and braced myself for the journey to Scotland Yard. Our cab advanced at a crawl, the driver doing his best to prevent the wheels sliding or the horse slipping. Holmes hummed to himself as he stared out the window into a dense fog, the street illuminated only by the misty glow of gas lamps. His stick tapped a rat-tat-a-tat rhythm on the floor of the cab, occasionally punctuated with forceful staccato thumps, which I imagined signaled that he'd cleared up some knotty aspect of a problem he'd been mulling over. Thankfully, the coffee had begun to invigorate me. My lethargy subsided and my mood improved.

After a lengthy and somewhat treacherous journey, our cab passed beneath the Whitehall Arch and deposited us at No. 4 Whitehall Place, Scotland Yard. Holmes paid the fare then pressed a guinea into the driver's hand and told him to wait.

"We shall be some while," said he. The driver flashed a grin, and then touched the brim of his cap before tucking the coin into a pocket of his waistcoat. A sudden gust breached our ulsters and set them flapping. Holmes pulled a flask from one of the deep pockets of his coat and handed it to the cabbie who took it with an appreciative nod.

Across the road, the carriage depot was all a bustle. Bucket boys darted here and there about their odorous work cleaning up after the horses. Cabbies called greetings to one another, some lively, others weary, but all, it seemed, with a lightness of spirit wholly alien to its neighbor. Scotland Yard, with its mellow red brick dressed in white stone, appeared imposing yet benign. However, no sooner had we crossed its threshold than a heaviness of spirit settled over me which I could not dispel. These precincts, despite every attempt at order and cleanliness, bore the ineradicable stain of human suffering and a palpable atmosphere of despair. There were few occasions that required me to set foot within these walls, and for that I was grateful. For, I imagined, the men, captive and captor alike, who daily passed in and out of its confines, must surely suffer a chronic and corrosive melancholy of spirit. How could it be otherwise?

The desk sergeant, a burly, ginger-haired fellow with bushy mutton chop whiskers, appeared to be dozing. Holmes tapped on his counter and the man started awake. He yawned, rubbed his eyes, then recognizing Holmes, jumped to his feet, muttered an apology, and wasted no time in ushering us to Inspector Lestrade. The policeman stood up from his desk and set aside the papers he'd been perusing before greeting us.

"Mr. Holmes. Dr. Watson. I must say, I am surprised to see you at this early hour."

The inspector was a little man, with what Holmes described, rather unkindly I thought, as rat-like features. His eyes were small, bright, and tended to dart about. That he was a restless fellow, always in need of expending excess energy, there was no doubt. Indeed, some part of his anatomy seemed always in motion. This morning however, he looked weary. My impression was that it was not so much the early hour, but that he, like I, had not slept well or perhaps at all. The dark stains beneath his eyes attested to it.

"My dear, Lestrade," said Holmes, "you look as if you've had a rough night."

"Indeed, I have," said the policeman, shaking his head before sinking again into his chair. "Of late, there have been some foul murders, each one worse than the last."

"So I've heard," replied Holmes.

"The one last night in Whitechapel, what a gruesome business that was. An unfortunate with her throat slit from ear to ear and her heart cut out. Whoever the blighter is, he took the heart out clean as a whistle and dressed her up again mantle and all. No one noticed until we found the heart in her reticule."

"If I can be of any assistance ..."

"I appreciate that Mr. Holmes," Lestrade said. "I expect I'll be calling on you sooner rather than later if things do not improve. Whenever there's another one like this, the rumors start. Saucy Jack is back. That's what they say. The Ripper is on the prowl again."

His typical arrogance had all but disappeared, replaced by an air of resignation. "Your message indicated you've been retained by Lord Silverpin as a private enquiry agent and wished to speak to me regarding the disappearance of his father. I fear there is not much I can tell you that you do not already know or have worked out for yourself."

"You flatter me, Inspector."

Lestrade heaved a weary sigh. "It's like this, Mr. Holmes. Two months ago, the Right Honorable Robert Henry, the Fifth Earl of Convarran, went missing. Well, I can tell you, Mr. Holmes, we were not happy to hear of that. Not with these vicious killings and the immigrant unrest festering in the East End. As you might expect, we are under constant pressure to untangle this affair and make an arrest. We have little to go on and no men to spare."

He directed our attention to the other desks in the room, each one bearing stacks of files requiring the attention of an inspector.

"I fear this will not end well for me or the Yard."

"I pray that is not so. Nevertheless, I beg you tell me all you know and all you suspect," said Holmes. "And you will have helped me immensely."

"Well, then," Lestrade said rising and retrieving two chairs from adjacent desks. "You both had best take a seat."

Holmes and I removed our hats and placed them with our sticks on a nearby desk. Once we had settled ourselves Lestrade opened his notebook and began his narrative.

"This is what we know. The Earl's train arrived at Paddington Station on schedule. The station master confirmed it. However, he did not recall anyone in particular exiting the train. Some idlers recalled that a carter was waiting for the train, and they were able to make a few shillings helping to unload the crates from the train onto the wagon. The carter dealt with them, so they did not see the Earl himself. The carter delivered the crates to the Egyptian Hall where they were stored. We have not been able to trace the carter. Whoever he was, he was not known at Paddington or the Egyptian Hall and his wagon bore no identifying marks. My men examined the crates and found nothing missing according to a packing list supplied to us by Lord Silverpin. The crates remained undisturbed at the Egyptian Hall until yesterday when Lord Silverpin had them removed to his Mayfair residence. What happened to the Earl after his train arrived at Paddington is unknown. The servants at the Mayfair residence swear he did not arrive there. The train returned to Whitchurch Station in Berkshire, but the Earl was not on board."

"What did the train crewmen say?"

"They did not see him board at Whitchurch. However, the shunter at Paddington believed he saw the Earl disembark in London. But he's a slow-witted boy and not wholly reliable."

"And the Hampshire estate?" Holmes asked.

"Highmount House is the Earl's country seat. House indeed! It's a bloody castle! There are thousands of acres surrounding the place. They have an army of servants, and there is a stream of people coming and going day in and day out, doing this, that, and the other."

"Dear me," said Holmes, "you'd need an army yourself to investigate the place."

"You've got that right enough, Mr. Holmes. I've been in communication with the local constabulary. The Highmount police searched the house and grounds as best they could. A man could disappear in that place, and no one the wiser. They found nothing to indicate foul play. They questioned the servants. No one saw or heard anything amiss."

"What about the Earl's associate, Sir Roger Trumbull? A scarab similar to the one discovered by Lord Silverpin and Lady Vivienne in the Earl's study was found on his body. Is that not so?" Holmes asked.

"Yes, that is so, and does seem to connect the two. Though, the events being so far apart in time is curious." Lestrade's expression turned sour. "The police surgeon says Sir Roger was alive when his hands were severed from his body."

"He died of shock, then," I said. "Acute physical trauma compounded by massive blood loss."

"Have you established any motive for Sir Roger's murder?" Holmes asked.

"He was alone in his study, the same as the Earl. His servants were out. It was their regular night off. We confirmed their whereabouts. The house was not disturbed, nothing was taken, which is why the butler did not find him until the next morning. We are going on with the theory that the killer is an Egyptian radical, or a group of radicals, opposed to the removal of cultural artifacts from Egypt and the sale of those artifacts to museums and private collectors. There have been threats made on the Earl's life and on Sir Roger's life in the past by such a group calling themselves The Protectors of the God-Kings. But nothing recent and none of their known members are presently in England."

"Trumbull had a rather unsavory reputation among professional Egyptologists," Holmes said. "He'd been accused of using underhanded and illegal means to acquire artifacts for the British Museum, everything from smuggling to buying from thieves. Might there be unknown members of these radical groups who have proceeded from threats to action?"

"Such things are not our province," said Lestrade. "That is international crime, and the government's concern."

"Just so," said Holmes. "However, I am here because my clients fear you have begun to embrace the notion that the Earl's disappearance is a publicity stunt, and they wish me to put you right."

Lestrade uttered a mirthless laugh. "I had not come to that determination, Mr. Holmes, but I dare say some days it makes more sense than any alternative we have investigated."

"My dear, Lestrade," Holmes said, "arriving at that conclusion is too simple-minded even for you."

"Now look here, Mr. Holmes!"

"What do my clients say to what you posit?"

"They won't have any of it!" Lestrade said bitterly. "Even though they don't deny the Earl's pulled such stunts before."

"Well, I think if a charade were the Earl's intention, he would have shown himself by now," Holmes replied tartly.

All the while we were talking with Lestrade, other inspectors were going to and from their desks, casting curious glances in our direction. Lestrade acknowledged a few of them with a raised hand. I wondered if the ones he ignored were rivals or if he did not consider them equals.

"Have you had any luck tracing Professor Emm?" I asked.

"No," said Lestrade. "We've had no communication from him. It seems his servants are on board pay which indicates he will be absent for some time. Let me tell you, Mr. Holmes, those servants of his are an unsavory looking lot. However, the professor's house appears to be in order, so there is little we can do except wait for him to return while questioning his associates regarding his whereabouts."

"Is it not possible that he also is missing?" said Holmes.

"We are coming around to that idea, Mr. Holmes. According to Lord Silverpin and his sister, the four men had a falling out in Egypt. Now two have disappeared, a third one is dead, and who is left but Mr. Cedric Matheson."

"According to my clients, Matheson is now *en route* to England. You may yet have an opportunity to apprehend the culprits if Matheson is the next target, unless of course his absence is a ruse, and he is responsible for these crimes. In any case, he must be warned."

A light came into Lestrade's eyes. "That's true."

"Good heavens, "I said. "One can hardly countenance such a thing. The man is world famous. Why, his name is a household word."

Holmes pressed on. "Have you any proof that Matheson was in India, as has been reported?"

"No, we don't," replied Lestrade.

"What about Lord Silverpin and his sister? Have you any reason to suspect their involvement?"

"No, and even if I did, I would tread very carefully before I made any accusations against them. You see my quandary, Mr. Holmes."

Holmes lips twitched in what might have been a ghost of a smile. "You do seem to be in a pickle," said he.

Lestrade frowned. "But as you suggest, we cannot overlook the lord and lady. One cannot ignore the fact that if their father were dead, Lord Silverpin would become the Sixth Earl of Convarran and inherit everything. As for Lady Vivienne, given the apparent devotion between the two, she would benefit greatly from her brother's ascension."

"I cannot believe Lady Vivienne could be involved in any way!" I protested.

"Really, Watson, such infatuation! Evil has been done for far less a prize, as you well know," Holmes replied acerbically.

I could not deny it, but I did not want to entertain the idea of her guilt. "That doesn't explain Trumbull or Emm," I countered.

"Perhaps, perhaps not," Holmes murmured. "However, once we have all the facts, we will know what role Trumbull and Emm played in this story. We are heading to Hampshire today, Inspector. Mayhap Watson and I can burrow in where you could not."

Lestrade shook his head ruefully. "I very much hope so, Mr. Holmes."

"We shall see, "said Holmes. "And now, before we take our leave of you, may we see the scarabs?"

The inspector hesitated. I expected him to quote police protocol denying us, but instead he shrugged. "I don't see the harm. If you can shed some light upon the matter that can only help us. If not, we've lost nothing." He stood. "Gentlemen, come with me."

We exited the inspectors' area and proceeded through a maze of hallways to the Yard's evidence room. We stopped before a thick wooden door. "Here we are," said Lestrade as he unlocked the door. The Evidence Room was filled with shelves that held countless boxes. Lestrade perused these closely and removed a box from a shelf and set it upon a table by the door.

"Here are the two scarabs." He lifted the lid from the box. We peered inside. There, alongside a leather-bound journal, were two ancient gems carved in the form of scarab beetles. The scarabs were approximately the size of a gold sovereign, wrought from a dark green, glass-like substance with the likeness of a beetle picked out in gold on the humped backs.

Holmes retrieved his lens from his pocket, picked up one of the scarabs and peered at it through the lens. He turned the scarab over, revealing the hieroglyphs carved on the underside. A strange expression animated his features such as I can only describe as perplexed but quickly resolved into astonishment.

"What is it, Holmes?" I asked. "What is the matter?"

He tossed me the scarab. Startled, I caught the beetle, gripping it tightly in my fist. What happened next, I can only explain as a result of lack of sleep and an overwrought imagination, neither of which I am prone to. Nevertheless, there is no other explanation. The scarab became uncomfortably warm. I opened my fingers. The scarab was on its back. As I gazed upon the hieroglyphs, they appeared to move, reshaping themselves into another combination, after which an intense feeling of dread assailed me. With a start and a shout, I dropped the scarab. Holmes snatched it before it fell to the floor and threw it back into the box.

"Do not worry, Doctor," Lestrade said, misreading my actions as clumsiness. "No harm done."

"Have you had these analyzed?" Holmes asked.

"I haven't," replied the Inspector.

"I suggest you do so as soon as possible. Enlist the services of the British Museum's Egyptology Department."

"Just what might we be looking for?"

"I'm not certain ... but I suspect whatever their findings they will help us in our investigations."

"If you say so, Mr. Holmes," said Lestrade with a curious look.

After retrieving his pocket notebook, Holmes reached into the box and tipped the scarabs onto their backs. He made a quick sketch of the hieroglyphs before picking up the leather-bound book.

"What is this?" he asked.

"That is the Earl's expedition journal," said Lestrade. "The Silverpins thought it might contain something that would help us. There is naught in it but accounts of expenses, packing lists, schedules, sketches, and notes pertaining to their excavations. No help at all."

Holmes thumbed through the pages, pausing occasionally to read more closely.

"May I borrow this for a short time?"

Lestrade shrugged. "It is of no use to us. Return it to your clients when you're done with it."

Holmes nodded and slid the journal into a pocket of his ulster.

As we walked back to the inspector's desk, Holmes had a twinkle in his eye when he said to the inspector, "I take it you give no credence to the talk of a pharaoh's curse?"

Lestrade gave Holmes a sharp look. "I am more inclined to believe that someone might wish to make it look like such a thing."

"Good man," said Holmes, clapping Lestrade on the back. "Now, shall we move on to Sir Roger's corpse?"

Lestrade did not accompany us to view Sir Roger's body. It lay in a parish mortuary, a small, chilly room situated below ground. I detected the odor of decay immediately, though an attempt had been made to mask the miasma with carbolic acid. The attendant urged us to hurry. The coroner's court had not ordered an autopsy and the body would shortly be removed by the undertakers to prepare it for burial. By all accounts, Sir Roger had been a robust man in life. In death, he was much diminished. Lifting the drape that covered his naked form, we beheld a body pallid, hirsute, and still showing signs of rigor. Though I had seen greater carnage in Afghanistan, the raw stumps of his arms still shocked me deeply. If Holmes was affected at all, he showed no sign of it. Instead, his curious gaze surveyed the body as if it were of no more consequence than a side of beef. After an anterior examination, with Holmes's assistance, I turned the body. There were no abrasions, bruises, or other injuries anywhere upon the corpse. We returned the body to its original position. I lifted his eyelids and found his eyes opaque. His facial features were smooth and untroubled. Amid the first signs of decay, his thick chestnut hair, touched with gray at the temples, retained its vibrancy. I replaced the drape.

"I cannot say with certainty whether Sir Roger fought against his attacker," I said. "Obviously, without his hands, I cannot examine the nails. However, given the otherwise unblemished condition of the body, I must conclude that he did not defend himself. I am sorry, Holmes, we have learned nothing here that will help us."

"On the contrary, Watson, we have learned much, though its meaning has yet to be revealed."

Chapter Three

We arrived at Paddington without a minute to spare. Holmes thrust the fare into our cab driver's outstretched hand, and we dashed to the train platform just as the conductor shouted his last call. He vigorously waved us aboard as steam billowed from the stack and swirled around the undercarriage. The whistle shrieked twice as we flung our bags on board and then swung up after them onto the slowly moving train. For better or worse, we were underway.

We were fortunate to be the only two passengers in our first-class compartment as this allowed us room to stretch our legs. I was grateful for this space, as well as the thick lap rugs, as my injured leg had a tendency to cramp. Unfortunately, ours was a "milk" train that stopped at every station along the route rather than the preferable Royal Mail express which would have carried us more quickly to our destination. I loaded my valise, medical bag, and the picnic hamper onto the overhead rack and settled into my seat.

During the first leg of our journey, we rode along in companionable silence, Holmes engrossed in a hoary, handwritten tome that had something to do with ancient Egypt, and I lost in thought about all that had transpired, which, to my mind, became stranger and more sinister with every new revelation. I had hoped the examination of Sir Roger's corpse might reveal additional clues not addressed in the police surgeon's report. But sadly, it was not to be. My speculation that the man had been drugged before being mutilated could not be substantiated as a postmortem had not been performed and there were no external indications noted – no lingering odor of chloroform upon the skin, no discoloration of tissue.

"Holmes," said I. "If Sir Roger's hands were amputated while he was conscious, and there is every indication that is so, then his manner of death was utterly barbaric."

Holmes raised his eyes from his book. "Indeed, exceedingly so."

"What kind of person would do such a thing? Could that person who is murdering and mutilating unfortunates be responsible for Sir Roger's death?"

"Highly unlikely, dear fellow, for many reasons, not the least of which is the mutilations have all been perpetrated upon unfortunate women. Those involved in our case are men – men of some renown and high standing. However, I must allow that in all situations, there is a personal element involved, as robbery has not been a motive."

"Yes, I see. And in our case, the men were all members of the same archaeological expedition."

"Just so," said Holmes. "Were you aware, Watson, that having one's hands cut off was a punishment for grave robbing in ancient Egypt?"

"No, I was not."

"There were two other punishments equally as gruesome – having one's head cut off, and being burned alive."

I shuddered. "That would seem to coincide with what we learned from Lestrade about the radicals opposed to the removal of cultural artifacts from ancient sites in Egypt. Could they – what did Lestrade call them – Protectors of the God-Kings? Could they be responsible?"

"It is possible of course. However, it could be that someone wishes to make Sir Roger's death appear to have been at the hands of radicals."

"Then, you do believe the Earl's disappearance and Sir Roger's murder are connected."

"I have no doubt of it, Watson."

"Because of the scarabs …"

"Yes," Holmes cut in. "That is one reason that connects them. And now you mention it, I observed your rather dramatic reaction to handling them. I take it you saw the hieroglyphs appear to move?"

"You saw it too! I thought it my imagination, but …"

"It's not magic, Watson. I suspect, some clever trick of the light interacting with the gem."

I felt he dismissed it all too easily. "How do you explain the heat that emanates from them and the anxiety they cause? I would even go so far as to say dread."

"A chemical in the stone itself, I should think. You recall the substance handled by hatters that drives them mad."

"Mercury, yes, but …"

"The substance from which the scarabs are made is much faster acting, obviously. There is little use in guessing. Guessing is a deplorable practice! We shall wait upon the results of the analysis before we embrace any theory."

He was right of course, but still it rankled. If he had experienced what I experienced, how could he remain so damnably unaffected? Irritated, I turned my attention to the outside world and gazed out the window at the countryside slipping by. Woods and fields, hedgerows, and orchards, still and peaceful in their season of rest; farms and hamlets, too, with smoke drifting from the household chimneys, all snug against winter's blast. Now and then, I caught a glimpse of cows wending their way to their milking barn; a shepherd moving his sheep along a narrow track with dogs dodging and nudging, keeping the herd moving. Despite Holmes's uncharitable view of crime in the countryside, these sights cheered me, and I decided a change in subject might yield a more rewarding conversation.

"What are you reading that engages you so deeply?" I asked.

"Ah," said he. "This book comes from the private collection of an acquaintance of mine, a gentleman who goes by the name of Scarabus. Not his real name, of course. He is a collector of eldritch lore who has knowledge beyond the academic study of the Egyptian pictographic language, and who has ferreted out the arcane uses to which these pictograms have been put.

"The hieroglyph or cartouche that appears on the scarab that Lestrade showed us is the name of Nophru-Ka. When the scarab is handled, as we did, a subtle change occurs. The hieroglyphs appear to change and reveal another name to which I can find no reference. There is a hint, perhaps, but I can make nothing of it."

"You amaze me, Holmes! I had no idea you could read hieroglyphics."

"They are a like a cipher, Watson. Few can read them, and even fewer penetrate their deeper meanings and uses.

"The name Nophru-Ka," Holmes tapped the volume in his lap, "appears nowhere else, but it is mentioned in Scarabus's book and has a rather sinister tale attached to it. This Nophru-ka is said to have communed with an alien god and obtained from this being, through terrible sacrifices, two objects: a strange, multi-faceted stone that allows one to see into all of time and space and a papyrus that opens a portal to another dimension, the place where this alien god exists. These objects are said to have been entombed with Nophru-ka in the Black Pyramid at Dahshoor."

"Surely, Holmes, you don't believe such fantasy has anything to do with this case?"

"It is not a matter of what you or I believe," Holmes replied. "It is what others down through the ages even unto our own time continue to believe. Think of the Grail, the Ark of the Covenant, and Atlantis! This may very well be what the Silverpins believe."

"What?" I cried. "They said nothing of this preposterous story when they spoke to us!"

"Did you not observe, Watson, the heads of their walking sticks when they arrived?"

"They were gold. Far beyond what either of us could afford," I said. "How has that anything to do with this legend?"

"The tops were Egyptian lotuses and beneath those on the collars were engraved two rings of writing: one of hieroglyphs, which I did not have an opportunity to decipher, and the other a Latin phrase: *Ex tenebris ad lucem.*

"From darkness into light," I repeated.

"Just so," said he. And 'from darkness into light' is the motto of a secret esoteric society which I have been able to ascertain goes by the name of The Golden Dawn."

"How by all that is wonderful did you ever discover that?"

"It is recently formed, and it is rumored that some of the most influential persons in the highest echelons of government and society are members. The Silverpins are members of this group, and it may be that the Earl, himself, is a member."

"Are you saying you believe that the Earl and his associates found these, these … objects … and brought them back to England? And that they are being abducted and killed by someone who is intent on retrieving these artifacts."

"Without more information, it is impossible to say. However, there is a connection, Watson, you may depend upon it, and that connection is what I must discover, the truth about the Silverpins, these artifacts, and if they are involved in something more far-reaching than the Earl's disappearance."

"It seems to me that you were investigating the Silverpins before they ever came to us," I surmised.

"You are as astute as ever, Watson. I can hide nothing from you. I admit at first it was idle curiosity. I was bored and the stories in the society pages offered an opportunity to engage my mind without resorting to what you so politely describe as my deplorable habit of self-poisoning. When I discovered a small, but singular connection leading to my brother, well, engage me it did. Upon further investigation, I discovered that the Silverpins are related not only to our Queen, but to the Russian Czar. The clothing they were wearing yesterday is not available in this country. In fact, it can only be purchased in Russia, and only by members of the Royal Court. To wit, they have recently been guests at the court of the Romanovs. You can be assured – if my brother Mycroft is involved – the government is likewise. He may suspect the Silverpins of some subterfuge and fears that they will take their knowledge to their kin, thus giving the Russians an advantage in the Great Game."

"Holmes!" I cried. "You make it sound as if you are a spider at the center of a great web of intrigue!"

"Hardly, Watson," said he as a grave expression transformed his countenance. "But, I can assure you that nothing about this case is commonplace. We have much to discover before we find our way to the center of this web and determine who is spinning it and why."

Despite Holmes's earnestness, these notions seemed to me far-fetched and hardly credible. Surely, there must be a simpler explanation. And, the simplest was not one I wished to entertain, but I felt it my duty to give voice to it, if only to keep the case on solid ground.

"I am loath to suggest this, Holmes, for I do not want to believe it, but might this not be a cunning ploy concocted by Lord Silverpin to obscure his machinations to obtain his family's wealth and property? It is clear that he and his father do not see eye to eye. Perhaps the Earl intended to pass over his son and bestow the inheritance upon another. Lord Silverpin would have the title, but little else."

"It is, of course, one of a number of scenarios, Watson. I believe our stay at Highmount House will prove or disprove that theory post haste."

Holmes had been smoking while we talked and the smoke from his black shag tobacco had turned the atmosphere poisonous. I threw open the window and the inrush of cold, bracing air quickly cleared the compartment of smoke. I waited a few moments before shutting the window and unpacking the contents of the hamper which I was relieved to find had suffered no damage due to our hurried boarding of the train. Mrs. Hudson, solicitous as always of our comfort, had prepared ham sandwiches on thick bread heavy with butter, hard-boiled eggs, some particularly excellent cheese, two generous slices of apple tart, and two small jars of sweetened tea.

While our landlady's exemplary lunch had fortified me, my feelings of uneasiness regarding the case had not, as I had hoped, been relieved by our conversation. Rather, my disquiet was further inflamed. Nevertheless, I found the rhythmic clacking of the train's wheels over the tracks threatening to lull me to sleep.

"Holmes," said I, "I had hoped that our meeting with Lestrade would provide some relief from this anxiety I am feeling, but it has not, and our earlier conversation has only served to overwhelm me with an ominous sense of foreboding. Surely, you must feel it, too?"

Holmes regarded me with a sardonic smile. "Let us review the facts, friend Watson. Doing so, I am sure, will set your mind at ease."

"There are few facts that shed any light on this affair," I replied testily.

"Well," said he, "let us first examine the Earl's peculiar behavior. On his return from Egypt, after abruptly cutting short the expedition, he locks himself away in his study for long hours, admits no one, and warns the servants away under threat of dismissal. He has not acted in this manner before. Why should he do so now?"

"Perhaps he was concealing something there. Perhaps gold or antiquities that he wished to keep hidden until he could take it to whomever he was dealing with. And consider the crates, Holmes."

"Yes. The crates are of singular interest. But, think: Why is it that the Earl reportedly wanted to make an early start to the station when his train in fact did not leave early, but at the appointed time? We know this because it arrived at Paddington as scheduled. There was no need to leave early from Highmount if the train was departing at its regular time."

"I cannot imagine. Unless," I continued, "he was drawn thus by some ruse and abducted during the journey."

For a moment, I was jubilant, certain I had hit upon the answer. But then the error in my reasoning struck me full force.

"No," I said, "impossible. The coachman would have been a witness and very likely a victim. Unless …"

"What have you deduced?"

"Unless the coachman was complicit, and the Earl never traveled to London."

"You have grasped some interesting threads, Watson. However, I think I can say with some certainty that the Earl did travel to London on his train, but perhaps not in the conventional sense."

"What do you mean?" I queried.

But Holmes, always reluctant to divulge his reasoning until the most propitious moment, would say no more.

Chapter Four

A southerly wind had swept away the clouds and brought with it clear skies and slightly warmer temperatures, turning yesterday's snow and ice to slush. By the time we chugged into Whitchurch station with its covered platform and tidy, well-maintained office, Holmes was restive, impatient to be away on the last leg of our journey. As instructed, he had telegraphed our itinerary before we departed Paddington. And, before the train had come to a full stop, he jumped out upon the platform casting his eyes about for the promised coach. As arranged, Lord Silverpin's coach awaited us. We were the only passengers to disembark and at our appearance on the platform, the Silverpins' coachman emerged from the station master's office and greeted us cordially.

"Staunton, isn't it?" Holmes inquired.

"Why, yes sir, it is," the man replied with an appreciative nod. "Take your seats, if you please, gentlemen, while I stow your cases."

"Excellent," said Holmes. "I trust you will proceed with all haste."

"Of course, sir," the coachman replied. "As fast as we are able under these conditions."

Holmes responded with a curt nod, and we climbed into the coach and covered our legs with the thick blankets we found on the seats. Lord Silverpin had also fitted the coach with a case containing glasses and a fine whiskey to ward off the cold and warm the inner man. We felt a slight jostle as Staunton ascended to his box. He snapped his whip, shouted "Get along, boys," to the horses, and the coach jolted forward.

The village of Highmount was in the county of Hampshire some seven miles from Whitchurch station. Our journey took us through farmland and over dirt roads and narrow tracks. On a dry, firm surface, a pair of strong Shire horses with an experienced driver might make the journey in two hours. But the trip took us over four hours, the slush and rutted roads slowing our progress considerably. Though Staunton did his best, and we suffered no damage, in many places, the coach rocked violently. Holmes, his nose again buried in his book, appeared oblivious to it all.

Suddenly, the horses began to neigh, and the speed of the coach increased. "Ah," said Holmes, still perusing his book, "our journey is nearing its end. The beasts have our destination in sight." Within a moment of his saying so came Staunton's thump upon the coach roof.

"Highmount House, gentlemen," he cried. "We're nearly there!"

I pressed close to the window as we turned into a long, winding drive. After some little time, I caught sight of the house, and it took my breath away. The place was large enough to hold half a village with room to spare.

"Good Lord, Holmes," I said. "It is a castle!"

He glanced up, an amused look on his face, as he marked his page and stuffed the book in his travel bag.

"You are in for a treat, Watson," said he. "The Earls of Convarran have occupied their country seat for centuries. I'm told the place is full of art and antiquities, and that the interior architecture is sublime."

A few minutes later, the coach halted. Staunton climbed down and ran to the house. He rang the bell and then hurried back to us. The coach door opened, and he unfolded the steps, allowing us to easily disembark.

"Mr. Holmes, Dr. Watson, if you'll go ahead, Mr. Jessup will see you inside and one of the footmen will be along shortly with your cases."

"Thank you, Staunton," Holmes replied. "Please stay nearby, I look forward to speaking with you later."

Staunton gave Holmes a curious look. "Begging your pardon, sir?"

Before more words could be exchanged, a stable boy trotted up and took charge of the horses. Staunton folded up the steps and slammed the coach door.

"Mr. Jessup is awaiting you at the door, gentlemen," he said before hurrying to the back of the coach to unload our bags for the footman.

Holmes gestured towards the door and the attendant butler. "Shall we, Watson?" And then quietly under his breath, he whispered to himself, "The adventure begins."

Jessup, unlike most butlers I had encountered, had the bearing and demeanor of a military man. Though completely dignified, he was a great bear of a man. I imagined he would give a commendable account of himself even in so base an altercation as a common street fight.

He informed us that Lord Silverpin and Lady Vivienne were otherwise engaged and would join us before dinner. As we followed him through Highmount's Great Hall, I found myself awestruck at the sight of its vaulted ceilings, arches, and massive hearth. Lustrous Persian carpets covered the parquet floors; ancestral portraits hung between the arches; stags' horns surmounted the lintels; and fig trees and ferns in Chinese urns sprouted here and there amongst the luxurious furnishings.

When I could tear my attention away from the splendor, I sensed Holmes champing at the bit to begin his investigation. Yet he said nothing as we approached the grand staircase. As we ascended, for just a moment, I glimpsed a woman, partially concealed by an arch, observing us. When our eyes met, she darted away and disappeared.

I was pleased to find that our rooms were adjoining suites connected by a comfortable sitting room. A nimble footman must have legged it up a back stair, for our bags had arrived ahead of us. Before departing, Jessup advised us on the protocols of the house. Within minutes of his departure, two maids appeared bearing trays loaded with tea pots, cups, saucers, and an assortment of savories and sweets. After filling our cups, they curtsied and left us to enjoy our tea.

We had only just finished when Jessup himself came to fetch us with word that Lord Silverpin awaited us in the Earl's study.

"Excellent!" said Holmes leaping up from his seat. "Lead on, Jessup!"

The butler inclined his head. "This way, gentlemen."

We followed Jessup down the grand staircase, across the Great Hall, through one of the arches to the Earl's study. This was no cozy space where one might tuck into a corner with a good book and pass a quiet hour or two. The room was cavernous with a massive window on one wall beneath which sat a large ornate desk. The place struck me as more of a museum with its glass cases, platforms, and plinths that displayed artifacts of dynastic Egypt. I noted several pharonic heads carved from basalt, a set of four luminous alabaster jars with animal-head lids, and a life-sized figure of a Nubian warrior brandishing a spear, among dozens of other pieces on display. There were also a number of photographs of the Earl's expeditions clustered together on a portable exhibition wall near the desk.

Watching us intently, Lord Silverpin reclined in a leather easy chair by the fireplace. He rose as we entered the room.

"Mr. Holmes and Dr. Watson, my Lord." Jessup bowed, first to Lord Silverpin, then to us, before departing.

"Your father's collection is quite remarkable," I said, gazing about in admiration.

"Feel free to examine it at your leisure, Doctor Watson. Please accept my apologies, gentlemen," he continued, "that we were unable to welcome you when you arrived."

"Think nothing of it," said Holmes.

Seeing no sign of his Lordship's sister, I asked, "Will Lady Vivienne be joining us?"

"Alas, no. We have experienced a most trying day."

"I'm sorry to hear that," I said, unable to keep the disappointment from my voice. "If I can be of assistance ..."

"Thank you, no, Doctor. My sister is not ill — only resting so she is refreshed for the evening."

Holmes sniffed the air like a bloodhound. "I detect an odor of beeswax and turpentine. This room has recently been cleaned."

"While we were in London, we sent word to the staff that guests were expected upon our return," Lord Silverpin explained. "We have all been beset by melancholy since father's disappearance. We've had no guests since, and your impending visit proved quite a distraction. The staff put all their energy into preparing for your arrival. They were quite agog at having Mr. Sherlock Holmes and Dr. Watson as guests. Needless to say, the housemaids scrubbed the place from top to bottom."

"There is no creature more destructive of evidence than a parlor maid!" Holmes declared. "If there were any finger marks, they have surely been rubbed away." Holmes waved a hand dismissively as he glared at the carpet. "Foot marks brushed away. Criminal!"

I suppressed a smile as I recalled my friend's rows with our landlady whenever she dared attempt to tidy our rooms.

Regaining control of himself, Holmes said in a more temperate voice, "Would you be so good as to show me exactly where the scarab was found?"

"Certainly," said Lord Silverpin, looking askance at Holmes. "Just about there." He indicated a spot on the carpet a few paces from the desk. The carpet's pattern was intricate and colorful, and I marveled that the scarab had been noticed at all and said as much.

"We did not see it," said Lord Silverpin. "But trod upon it."

Holmes dropped to his knees, convex lens in hand. After carefully examining the surrounding area, he stood and went to the desk. The desktop held what one might expect: an inkwell and pen, blotter, letter opener, paper weight, a lamp, and a few well-thumbed books on Egyptology. After examining the surface of the desk, Holmes placed a hand upon the central drawer.

"May I?"

"You may, sir" Lord Silverpin replied.

Holmes pulled open the drawer and assessed the contents which appeared to be nothing more than stationary, sealing wax, and other sundries. Other drawers contained only bits and bobs of ephemera, ceramic shards, and scraps of what looked to be papyrus paper covered in faded images and hieroglyphs. The last drawer on the bottom right refused to open and no amount of jiggling could free it.

"Wait a moment." Lord Silverpin joined Holmes at the desk. "There is a combination." He grasped the drawer handle, a rosette with six petals, which he turned three times to the left, then five times to the right, then seven times to the left. The drawer opened as easily as if it had been greased. We peered inside. Holmes examined the empty drawer inside and out with his lens.

"What did this drawer contain?"

"It is where we found our father's expedition journal. The police have it."

"As it happens," said Holmes, "Inspector Lestrade has sent it along with me to return." Holmes removed the journal from the pocket of his coat and placed it in the drawer.

"Thank you," said Lord Silverpin. "It was of no use to him then?"

"Unfortunately, no," said Holmes. "I notice there is no correspondence, personal or business."

"It is our father's habit to burn any communications of which he had no further need. Important papers would have been secured in his vault," Lord Silverpin said.

I could only imagine the effect this knowledge would have upon my friend – he who had a horror of disposing of any document lest it at some time prove useful . "Pray, where is this vault located?" asked Holmes.

Lord Silverpin moved to a bookcase to the right of the desk whereupon he performed a combination of movements with his hands which caused the case to swing away from the wall, revealing a walk-in vault, its formidable looking door secured by a combination lock.

"Have you examined the vault contents?" Holmes asked.

"We have. There are estate ledgers, some coin and notes, bills of lading, and a few small antiquities. You may examine the contents yourself if you wish."

"I may wish to do so later, thank you," said Holmes, scrutinizing the vault with a cracksman's eye.

There was a discreet knock at the door. We turned to find Jessup crossing the room, bearing a silver salver with a calling card upon it. He bowed. "Your presence is required, my Lord."

Lord Silverpin picked up the card, glanced at it, and then slipped it into a pocket of his waistcoat.

"Where have you put our visitor, Jessup?"

"In your study, my Lord."

"Gentlemen, if you will excuse me."

"May I continue my examination of the room?" Holmes asked.

Lord Silverpin pressed the bookcase firmly back in place. I noted a slight hesitation before he replied, "By all means, Mr. Holmes, you may continue. In my absence, Jessup will remain to assist you."

"That is quite unnecessary, my Lord," Holmes said. "I do not wish to keep Mr. Jessup from is duties. Dr. Watson can provide all the assistance I require."

A slight frown bent Lord Silverpin's lips as he glanced first toward the bookcase, then at Jessup.

"Very well," he said. "My sister and I look forward to both of you joining us at dinner."

"I must decline your generous invitation," said Holmes. "I find I am exhausted from our journey." He touched his forehead. "I fear a headache coming on. If I am to interview your servants on the morrow, I must rest. Kindly convey my deepest regret and sincerest apologies to Lady Vivienne. Of course, Dr. Watson is a scintillating conversationalist; I am sure you and your sister will find that he more than makes up for my absence."

I felt my face flush at Holmes's praise. However, my pleasure was short-lived as a look of what I took to be disappointment flitted across Lord Silverpin's features, though he quickly recovered his amiable demeanor.

"We are sorry to hear it," Mr. Holmes. "Our little party will be the poorer for your absence." He turned to me. "I intend no slight to you, Dr. Watson."

"None taken, your Lordship," I replied, wondering what Holmes was up to. Most likely he was not ready to reveal his thoughts and did not wish to find himself in a position where our hosts would quite naturally attempt to draw him out. On the other hand, it was altogether possible that Holmes had already solved the case but had not yet gathered sufficient evidence to support his conclusion.

"We shall have our housekeeper instruct Cook to send up your dinner," Lord Silverpin said.

"Most kind, but unnecessary," Holmes replied. "Our tea was sufficient sustenance. I shall need no other this evening."

"As you wish, Mr. Holmes."

After Lord Silverpin departed with Jessup, Holmes glanced at the door to the study.

"Close that door and lock it would you, old man?"

I did as requested and returned to my friend's side. He stood for a long-time gazing at the wall of photographs, and then he paced around the perimeter of the room closely examining walls, moldings, and hearth surround. Apparently not finding what he was looking for, he let forth an exasperated exhalation.

"Where can it be?" he said to himself.

"What are you looking for, Holmes? Tell me and I will help."

Suddenly, Holmes gave a muted cry of triumph.

"Of course, why did I not realize before?"

He bounded to the bookcase and replicated the motions Lord Silverpin had used. I stood astounded as the bookcase swung away from the wall. He examined the lock mechanism, and then pushed the bookcase back into place.

"It is a Chubb Detector," he muttered to himself, frowning. "Daren't try without the key. Hum. We shall have to see …" he trailed off as he paced, chin sunk upon his chest. After a lengthy pause, he looked up and addressed me in a low voice: "I'm sure you have realized by now that the Silverpins have not told us all they know of this business. It is suggestive, is it not, that the primary servants go about their duties armed, and as I'm sure you've noticed just now, Lord Silverpin is also armed. What do you make of that?"

Chapter Five

I confess, I had not noticed that our hosts and their servants carried concealed weapons upon their persons, but I did not say as much to Holmes.

"They are in fear of something. Most likely they anticipate being set upon by the same villains responsible for the outrage upon the Earl."

We had returned to our rooms and Holmes had settled into one of the easy chairs, his long legs stretched toward the fire. He had changed into his dressing gown and was smoking his cherry wood pipe.

"Did you notice the woman? When we first came up with Jessup, she was about to enter the Great Hall."

I had been dressing for dinner and just finished with my tie before returning to our sitting room with my evening shoes. "A servant, surely. When she saw us, she turned and disappeared into one of the rooms."

"No servant beneath the butler or the housekeeper would dare be seen in that section of the house when the family and their guests are active."

"No doubt the reason she fled at the sight of us. She feared reproach from Jessup."

"Except, Watson, Jessup saw her and said nothing. She did not make for the servants' door, but fled in a direction where there was the highest probability of her being seen. She easily could have gone in the opposite direction and avoided exposure entirely."

"You make too much of it, Holmes. We startled the woman; she acted on impulse without considering the consequences. Jessup did not wish to cause a scene in front of guests. No doubt he or the housekeeper will take the woman to task later in the servants' hall."

"Did you observe the way she was dressed?"

"I barely caught sight of her before she disappeared."

"She was not dressed as a servant. She wore a foreign costume. When you dine with the Silverpins, do your best to discover who she is."

I sighed as I dropped into the other easy chair. The identity of this woman was yet another of Holmes's obsession with trifles. As I slipped on my shoes, Holmes took a deep draw on his pipe, and turned toward me.

"Watson, dear friend, I have another little assignment for you."

I groaned inwardly. While I would never refuse to assist Holmes, at times his requests were not the easiest to fulfill, and more than once had landed me in uncomfortable situations.

"What is it you want me to do?"

Holmes smiled sardonically. "Steady on, old fellow, it is nothing difficult. In fact, it is right up your street. While you are dining with his Lordship and Lady Vivienne, draw them out about their time in Egypt. They were born there and lived there for some years before the family returned to England."

I finished tying my shoes and stood to don my evening coat. "I will do my best, Holmes, but I cannot imagine how I can politely broach the subject, let alone inquire into such a personal and quite likely delicate matter. Did you not tell me the Earl's wife perished soon after their return to England having contracted some hideous disease while they were living in Egypt?"

"Just so."

"That is a difficult request, Holmes." I snatched up my cigarette case from the table and deposited it in my waistcoat pocket. "I will see what I can do," I replied rather testily.

"Do your best, Watson, do your best," said he, closing his eyes, steepling his fingers, and resting his head upon the chair back.

"It would be helpful if you told me exactly what it is you want to know. Otherwise, I'll be blundering about in the dark."

"If I knew that, old man, I would simply ask."

I was in a rather less than amiable mood as I descended the grand staircase. I experienced a moment of consternation when I realized I could not recall where we were to gather before dinner. However, my anxiety was short lived as a footman appeared and guided me to a drawing room where I found Jessup. He fetched me a sherry while assuring me that Lord Silverpin and Lady Vivienne would join me in a few moments. In the meantime, I was free to examine the distinguished collection of art that adorned the walls. I sipped my drink as I admired the paintings, many of which appeared to depict events from the English Civil War. I had been so engaged for at least twenty minutes when a footman entered the room. He exchanged a whispered communication with Jessup, and then quickly departed. A moment later, the second dinner gong sounded.

"Dinner will be served in twenty minutes, Dr. Watson. May I escort you to the dining room? His Lordship and her Ladyship will join you there shortly." Jessup started toward the door, and I followed, but then he stopped and turned to face me. His expression was such that I surmised his emotions must be in turmoil.

"Whatever is the matter, Jessup?" I asked, somewhat taken aback.

"I am sorry, sir. I did not intend to alarm you. However, I feel I must personally apologize to you, Dr. Watson, for your reception and subsequent treatment. It has been a topsy-turvy day. The household is seldom so disordered."

"There is no need to apologize, Jessup. We all have such days."

Jessup bowed. "Most understanding of you, sir."

Without knowledge of the day's events, I could only wonder what had discomfited Jessup and the household to a degree that would cause him to feel it necessary to make such a confession to a guest.

As we entered the dining room, I could not help but remark upon the immense portrait of King Charles I and his horse that dominated the room. Upon seeing the monarch who had been so cruelly executed at the hands of the traitor Cromwell, my thoughts turned immediately to the curious case of the Musgrave Ritual. Holmes credited the solving of that case with earning him a sterling reputation amongst the aristocracy, and well it should have for in addition to solving two strange disappearances, he had uncovered the ancient crown of the kings of England hidden by Charles's royalist allies. However, it was equally true, as Holmes often reminded me, that while being employed by the aristocracy was often quite lucrative, any misstep or failure on his part could prove equally disastrous and ruinous to his reputation. I could only pray that this outré and enigmatic case did not prove to be his undoing. My reminiscence was interrupted when Lord Silverpin and Lady Vivienne appeared.

Holmes and I had been unsure if we would be dining with our hosts, but we had packed our whites just in case and a lucky thing, too. Even so, I was little dressed compared to Lord Silverpin whose evening attire was the latest in Savile Row fashion, cut from the finest silk, and most cunningly fitted, while my own clothing, though of good quality and impeccably maintained, had been in service for some time.

Lady Vivienne, on her brother's arm, greeted me warmly. I was momentarily struck dumb at the sight of her. Her slender form was encased in a shimmering gown of dark green velvet embroidered with gold thread and accented with hundreds of tiny green and gold crystals. She wore a fabulous necklace of glowing emeralds set in gold. A matching tiara nestled in her ebony hair piled high with tiny twists and curls framing her perfectly symmetrical face. Her perfume was heavenly, though the scent still eluded me.

The footman had drawn out the chairs, and at Lord Silverpin's command we took our seats: he at the head of the table; his sister opposite him, in the royal fashion; and I in the middle to his right. After thanking our hosts again for their kind invitation, I inquired whether anyone else would be joining us."

For a moment, Lord Silverpin looked perplexed. "Oh, the gentleman who called this afternoon. No, his presence here was purely business."

"I beg your pardon," I said. "I meant the lady we encountered when we arrived."

Lord Silverpin and Lady Vivienne exchanged a puzzled look.

"I am sorry, Dr. Watson, there are no other guests in the house at present," said Lady Vivienne.

"I am mistaken then," I said. "She was wearing some foreign attire and I assumed …"

Lady Vivienne laughed softly. "Now we understand. You saw Neferuptah. She is a retainer, our old nursemaid. She cared for us when we were children in Egypt."

Ha! Holmes had been wrong; the woman was a servant.

"When you left Egypt, did your nurse not wish to remain there with her family?"

"Neferuptah had no family, Dr. Watson, or so she said. At any rate, we had become attached to her, and she to us. When we returned to England, she came with us. She has never expressed any desire to return to Egypt."

While we conversed, Jessup filled our wine glasses before a footman came around with a pleasing cream of parsnip soup.

"It is a shame," Lord Silverpin said, "that Mr. Holmes is indisposed. We hoped he would expound on his thoughts so far upon the disappearance of the Earl. We realize, of course, that much time has passed and there may be little evidence of what occurred, and he has only just begun to investigate, but by all accounts, Doctor, it is said that Mr. Holmes can make much of very little."

"That is true," said I. "However, he is absolute in his refusal to speculate beyond the facts. He will want to collect as much data as possible before offering an opinion. However, I believe I can tell you that, after speaking with Inspector Lestrade, Mr. Holmes is strongly considering Egyptian radicals as the possible perpetrators."

"Indeed," said Lady Vivienne. "What evidence has he to support this theory?"

"The manner of Sir Roger's death is significant. I understand from Holmes that having one's hands cut off was one of a number of gruesome ways in which grave robbers were punished in ancient Egypt."

"Quite so," said Lord Silverpin. "Yet, one must ask, if the intent of these radicals is to force the return of the Earl's collection to Egypt, and his abduction is to gain a hostage to bargain with, why has there been no communication?"

I did not know how to answer. In desperation, I replied, "Perhaps some aspect of their plan has gone awry."

"You mean that our father is dead," said Lady Vivienne.

"No, I … I am sorry. I did not mean to suggest …"

Lord Silverpin forestalled my blundering with an upheld hand. "Do not distress yourself, Doctor. It is a possibility that we must consider, no matter how unpleasant."

"Of course," I said. "I pray we find him alive."

"I mean no slight to Mr. Holmes," said Lady Vivienne. "However, I do not see how murdering poor Sir Roger and abducting Professor Emm serves these creatures' purpose unless their purpose is solely retribution."

"Quite possibly," I said weakly. I was feeling completely out of my depth. Holmes had confided nothing to me, and I now bitterly regretted my rashness in attempting to speak for him, for, truthfully, I hadn't the slightest notion to which of his theories he presently gave the most weight. Holmes certainly would not have ventured to say unless he was close to a certainty of his conclusion.

To my great relief, we had progressed to the dinner entrée. Conversation ceased for a time as Jessup once again filled our wine glasses and we proceeded to dine, I in appreciative silence, on a succulent cut of pork, tender and skillfully sauced.

"And what of the scarabs, Doctor. Do they offer any clue?"

I was not sure how to reply to Lady Vivienne's question, for surely if the Silverpins had handled the scarabs they would have experienced the same strange phenomena that Holmes and I experienced. I could only hope I was not revealing something that Holmes wished to keep to himself, but rather than stand mute, and feeling more than a little warm from the wine, I plunged ahead.

"Well," said I, "we had a rather strange experience with those scarabs." I described the heat I felt emanating from the stone, the hieroglyphs that appeared to move and change, and the intense anxiety I experienced afterward.

"How unusual," said Lady Vivienne glancing at her brother. "What does Mr. Holmes make of it?"

"Holmes believes there is a rational explanation. He suggested Inspector Lestrade have the scarabs analyzed at the British Museum. Hopefully, there will be a report waiting when we return."

"We shall be most interested to hear the results," Lord Silverpin replied.

I had divulged as much information as I deemed prudent. Though I must admit, it was hard going for me to evade their questions as both Silverpins were charming, exceedingly charismatic, and their combined personal beauty was more than a little overwhelming.

We had worked our way leisurely through seven dinner courses that were so expertly prepared and attractively presented that every bite had been an absolute delight. I imagined my waistcoat would be straining at its buttons. But on the contrary, I felt eminently satisfied and not over-full in the least. When we had finished dessert, a glorious apple tart I was told was their cook's specialty, Jessup brought a bottle of port and Lord Silverpin suggested we repair to the game room.

"Oh, dear, how awkward," said Lady Vivienne. "Generally, we play whist, but without Mr. Holmes, we are three-handed."

I saw my opening. "Perhaps," said I, "in place of cards, you could tell me something of your time in Egypt. I have never been and would dearly like to know more of the country and its people."

Lord Silverpin smiled. Lady Vivienne clapped her hands together and laughed delightfully. I laughed, too, completely taken in by her enthusiasm.

"As the children of an Egyptologist, our time there was one of myths, ancient mysteries, and a hair-raising adventure or two," said Lord Silverpin. "Shall we regale you with a few tales, Doctor?"

"I insist upon it," I cried.

And so, we passed the rest of the evening quite pleasantly as I listened spellbound to tales of their Egyptian childhood in Cairo and on the plains of Giza. Lord Silverpin began by describing how, on a dare, they and their nursemaid had shut themselves in a burial crypt with a mummy as their companion. All through the night, Neferuptah, by the light of a single candle, told them stories of the ancient gods.

On another occasion, while boating on the Nile, their small craft was forced into some debris by the wake of a bigger boat. Their vessel capsized, forcing them to swim to shore. Pursued by crocodiles, they narrowly escaped being devoured.

Lady Vivienne told the final story and the most alarming. They, being children of an adventurous and headstrong nature, had disobeyed their father's orders never to go into the Old City alone. Disobeying in order to partake of the wonders of the marketplace with all its exotic wares and entertainments, they, suddenly and without warning found themselves pursued by slavers. They were captured by these villains and believed themselves lost before they were boldly rescued by their resourceful nursemaid and a group of angry fellahin.

"Good, Lord!" I exclaimed. "Quite astonishing!"

"Indeed," said Lord Silverpin.

"I dare say, your nursemaid's behavior was certainly remarkable. Were your parents not quite alarmed?"

Lady Vivienne laughed her musical laugh. "If they had known what we got up to, I'm sure they would have been."

"Of course, Neferuptah took great care of us, and would never have let any harm come to us," said Lord Silverpin. "She is extraordinary and very proud. It was said by the fellahin that she has the blood of the ancient pharaohs in her veins."

A moment later, I heard the clock in the Great Hall chime midnight. Realizing the lateness of the hour and that I needed rest if I was going to be of any use to Holmes the following day, I declared my need for sleep and thanked the Silverpins for an extremely entertaining evening. They, too, were surprised by the late hour and determined to go immediately to their beds. We left the game room together and passed into the Great Hall where I followed them as they walked arm-in-arm up the grand staircase. At the top of the stairs, we parted company as they turned left and I to the right.

As I came to Holmes's door, I knocked lightly and listened for any sign that he might be awake. But hearing nothing and receiving no answer, I went on to my own room. Yet, as I prepared for bed, I felt compelled to report to Holmes what I had learned. I opened the connecting door and found the room dark. The gas jets had been turned off, forcing me to retrieve matches from my coat to light a candle. Half-dressed and in stockinged feet, I crossed our sitting room and rapped on Holmes's bedroom door. When again no answer came, I started to return to my own room. I could not understand it; under normal circumstances, my friend was the lightest of sleepers. When on a case, he was positively an insomniac. Dash it all, he needed the information I'd gathered sooner rather than later. Again, I rapped, loudly enough to wake him before opening the door and calling his name.

"Holmes, are you awake, old man?"

I held the candle aloft. The room was empty, his bed not slept in. Holmes was gone.

Chapter Six

I awoke in my chair to a fire burned low. Holmes sat across from me reading. It was early enough that light had not yet begun to seep in behind the curtains and the maid had not yet been in to make up the fire.

"Holmes! Where were you last night?" I cried whilst vigorously rubbing my hands together to warm them.

Holmes held a finger to his lips and placed the book he'd been reading in the pocket of his dressing gown. His hearing was as keen as a fox's and a moment later, I too, heard the footsteps in the hall, followed by a discreet tap before the door opened.

"Don't be alarmed, my dear," Holmes said, waving in the maid. "Strange beds often make for early risers."

"Yes, sir," the girl said averting her eyes and dropping a curtsy. She made up the fire in a trice and was gone just as quickly.

Holmes shifted his position to face me. I noticed he grimaced as he did so, and he clutched his arm.

"Have you injured yourself?" I asked.

"I was attacked," said he, undoing his nightshirt to reveal where the dark stain of a bruise had formed. "I was struck with a heavy instrument, a cudgel, I suspect."

"Good lord!" I said. "Let me get my bag."

"Nothing is broken, though I fear my shoulder is dislocated. If you wouldn't mind …"

I positioned myself behind him and set my knee against his back. Taking hold of his shoulder, I applied the needed pressure and pulled. In an instant, my friend went quite pale, and I feared he might lose consciousness.

"This is an outrage," I said. "How did this happen? Who has attacked you?"

"The house is being watched, Watson," said he with an effort.

"Watched! By whom?"

"I don't know yet. I was attacked because I stumbled upon one of them in the dark. I can only hope my blunder does not set in motion events we cannot successfully counter."

My heart racing, I asked, "Do you anticipate an attempt to abduct the Silverpins?"

"That is of course a possibility. However, I suspect an attempt has already been made and repelled; hence our clients and their servants going about armed. There is something here these scoundrels are after. And so long as these watchers believe this object is here, we are all in danger. I fear they are biding their time until an opportunity arises to seize the item."

"Have you any idea what they are after?"

"I'm beginning to form a hypothesis. I expect that further reading of the Earl's journal will shed more light upon the matter. But it is instructive to note that every door and window at Highmount has been inscribed with wards."

"Wards?"

"Yes. In this case, symbols of the goddesses Bast, Nepthys, and Isis, with the purpose of repelling evil, deterring thieves, and protecting those who live within."

"I had not noticed."

"No, of course not. They are cleverly concealed."

"But the Earl's journal, Holmes? I dare say, I don't see how that can be of any help."

"Oh, it is of the very greatest importance, Watson. Indeed, the whole case revolves on what it may reveal."

"Lestrade …"

"Did not have it. What Lestrade had is the Earl's expedition journal. What I have purloined is the Earl's private journal."

My mind was reeling. "But how did you know?"

"Tut, tut, Watson. Do you not recall the photograph in the Earl's study? He is in his tent and a journal with a leather cover with an Eye of Horus engraved upon the cover is on the table before him. Obviously, it is not the expedition journal because we have seen it. That journal is plain leather with no decoration. My obvious conclusion is that there are two journals."

He removed the book in discussion from his pocket and held it up for me to see.

"I found it concealed in a hidden compartment, along with this key, in Lord Silverpin's escritoire. Tonight, when I have an opportunity to read more of it, we may very well discover what it is our villains are after and thereby who they are."

"Holmes!" I cried. "You are guilty of theft!"

"So it is, Doctor. But tell me: what other recourse have I when our clients keep secrets from us?"

"You must then find out why they are lying to us," I declared.

"Not so much lying," said Holmes. "Rather, omission. What little they have told us, I dare say, is true. However, it is only the first layer of the onion! I have uncovered much that will soon make this affair plain. But now we must see what we can glean from the servants. I doubt it will be much. Yet, people don't disappear into thin air. Someone knows something, whether they are aware of it or not, and it is down to us to find that person."

It was a great deal to take in and had momentarily caused me to forget my grievance. I pushed away all other concerns and confronted my friend.

"You might have told me, Holmes. That would have saved me a night in this chair."

"Dear old, Watson. Your vigil was completely unnecessary, yet I am chastened by your distress. I could not tell you lest your concern give away the game. I did not and still do not know with certainty who our allies are in this affair and who opposes us."

I muttered something about trust and being ready in case I was needed, and then, recalling my original purpose, I reminded my friend of the task he had given me.

"Capital!" he cried. "Tell me all that you have learned. Leave nothing out."

I first took pride in informing him of his error. "It seems I was right in my deduction of the foreign woman, and you were wrong. She is indeed a servant. Her name is Neferuptah and she is a retainer, the Silverpins' Egyptian nurse who cared for them when they were children."

"Did she dine with you?"

"Certainly not!"

"What business did she have in the house?"

"I haven't the slightest idea."

"Then you have learned very little," said he. "There are retainers' cottages nearby. If she were a servant, she would live there and not have rooms in the castle."

"I'm sure there is a simple explanation," I said, smarting from his rebuke.

"Pray, what might that be?"

"I don't know," I said hotly.

"Well, then. Proceed with your report."

While Holmes packed his pipe with tobacco and lit it with a brand from the fire, I, still fuming, reluctantly reported our dinner conversation, leaving out my blunder concerning Egyptian radicals. Finally, I recounted the Silverpins' childhood adventures with their nurse. Holmes listened intently to my report, puffing gently on his pipe.

"Thank you, Watson. I'm sure you did your best, old man."

Really! The arrogance of the man!

"Now, tell me — did anything happen during the evening that struck you as odd or out of place. Anything at all?"

His egotism grated and I started to say so but then decided the best course was to hold my tongue. Argument would do no good in the long run.

"Your brow is creased," Holmes observed. "Something has occurred to you."

"It is less than trivial," I replied rather sulkily. "It is of no consequence at all."

"Come, come," Holmes said. "Out with it."

"Dinner was delayed, and Jessup apologized to me personally, saying it had been a topsy-turvy day and the house was rarely so disordered. And Lady Vivienne wore a tiara."

I had noted it at the time, yet it was a small thing and given Holmes's earlier statement about the Silverpins' penchant for free thinking, my recognition of it had been fleeting.

Holmes's eyes brightened. "Did she?" he said. "As if she were a married woman?"

"Not so surprising," I replied. "You said yourself the Silverpins often defy convention. And come to think of it, why shouldn't she wear a tiara in her own home, if she wishes. You should have seen her, Holmes, she was magnificent."

"You have me there, Watson," said he with the quickest of smiles. "You're becoming quite the iconoclast! By the by, what time have you?"

I checked my pocket watch. "Half eight," said I.

"Let us dress and go down and see if breakfast has been laid on."

A few minutes before nine, we descended the grand staircase into the Great Hall, where Holmes drew my attention to a portrait of Robert Henry, Fifth Earl of Convarran and his Countess, the Silverpins' parents.

"Note the family resemblance," he remarked looking at me steadily. As I gazed at the Earl and Countess, their fair skin, blonde and auburn hair, blue eyes, and not to mention the Earl's rather prominent nose and the Countess's bulging eyes, I realized that Holmes was having me on.

"With Lord Silverpin—and Lady Vivienne—there is no family resemblance to the Earl and the Countess," I declared.

"My point exactly."

"A person's attributes may skip a generation," I replied rather testily. "It is well known."

"Indeed," said Holmes with a sweep of his arm. "Cast your eyes over generations of this family and you will not find one who this brother and sister resemble. Nor will you find any evidence of twins on either side."

"What are you getting at Holmes? Surely, you're not suggesting …"

He shushed me as we approached the dining room.

Upon entering, we found Jessup, a footman, and a maid engaged in arranging the serving dishes on a sideboard laden with a plenitude of eggs, bacon, sausage, toast and jam, and kedgeree. Assailed with such delightful aromas, my stomach immediately set up a loud appeal. The footman and maid departed while Jessup prepared our coffee service before bowing and taking his leave.

I filled my plate to nearly overflowing while Holmes, as was his wont when on a case, took only a little toast with marmalade. Lost in thought, he sipped his coffee and nibbled at his toast while I ate heartily. I have always found simple, filling food to be a breastplate against anxiety and after Holmes's earlier revelations of his attack and the presence of the watchers, there was much to be anxious about.

My appetite fully satisfied, I sat back in my chair and placed my napkin on the table. As I poured myself another cup of coffee, Holmes withdrew a photograph from his coat and held it out for me to view.

"By Jove," said I, dropping my voice to a whisper at his admonishment. "Is that Lady Vivienne got up like an Egyptian?"

He turned over the photograph revealing a date written upon the back in faded ink.

I nearly dropped my cup. "Good, lord! Does that mean what I think it means, Holmes?"

"I should be very much surprised if it doesn't," he replied, slipping the picture back in the pocket of his coat. "I found it amongst the Earl's possessions."

Chapter Seven

My brain teemed with questions I wanted to ask my friend, not the least of which was what would be done about the malefactors watching the castle; and how would we eliminate the danger they posed. But before I could voice my concerns, Jessup arrived to inform us that a drawing room had been made ready where we might interview the servants.

"Excellent!" said Holmes. "We shall begin immediately."

By teatime, Holmes had questioned most of the servants. This was a feat considering there were sixty or more indoor servants as well as the outdoor staff of coachmen, grooms, stable boys, gardeners, farm hands, and several assistants. He accomplished this by gathering the staff in small groups according to their occupations. He spoke to the primary servants individually; as well as a few individuals who we discovered had not been interviewed by the police.

The interviews went surprisingly quickly, though they were nonetheless tedious, as invariably the answers to our questions were met with impassive looks and unwavering avowals that nothing out of the ordinary had been seen or heard. How Holmes endured such a monotonous recitation without succumbing to utter frustration was beyond me. The servants' answers were remarkably consistent with what we'd already been told by the Silverpins and Inspector Lestrade and we learned little more of the Earl's movements on the day of his disappearance. This shouldn't have come as a surprise, I suppose, as servants who worked for these old aristocratic families and particularly those who had been in long service were, for the most part, unstintingly loyal and unlikely to say anything they considered to be revealing of the private lives of their employers.

"Who is left?" asked Holmes, his voice heavy with weariness and *ennui*.

I ran my finger down Jessup's list of staff. "Just two, thank goodness," I replied. "Jim Gladney, a groom, and Emily Purcell, a scullery maid."

My pronouncement elicited an audible sigh of relief from Holmes. "At last," said he. "Let us hope that at the end of our quest we are rewarded with joy."

"It is likely to be more of the same, Holmes."

"Quite possibly," said he, "but we must leave no stone unturned. Summon Miss Purcell, if you please."

I rang for Jessup. The butler appeared almost immediately.

"Jessup, would you send for Miss Purcell and Mr. Gladney. I believe they are the last two."

"Very good, sir."

We didn't have long to wait before there was a light tap at the door. Jessup stepped in, followed by the scullery maid. Emily Purcell was a rather timid looking creature in a mob cap that covered her russet curls. The tendrils of hair that escaped her cap were damp and clung to her forehead. Her eyes, when she raised her gaze from the floor, which was seldom, were a striking electric blue. She smelled of citrus. Doubtless she'd been about her washing when she was summoned. Her maid's costume, shielded by a voluminous apron, bore the stains of her profession, the folds of which she now twisted nervously between reddened fingers. She was a tiny little thing and looked no more than a child. However, from Jessup's staffing manifest, I knew her to be seventeen years of age.

"Miss Purcell," Jessup announced. The scullery maid dropped a curtsy.

"Thank you, Jessup," said Holmes.

"Certainly, sir. Mr. Gladney is waiting in the hall. You may call for him when he is required."

Jessup bowed and made to withdraw.

"Jessup, before you go, tell me, how long have you been employed at Highmount?"

"I've been employed here since November of '89, sir."

"What became of your predecessor?"

"I'm sure I cannot say, sir."

"Thank you, Jessup. That will be all."

Jessup bowed and withdrew, closing the door behind himself.

Miss Purcell, looking quite uncomfortable, remained standing where Jessup had left her.

"Do sit down, Miss Purcell," I said in what I hoped was a kindly voice, indicating the chair across from Holmes.

"Thank you, sir," she said and curtsied again. Before taking her seat, she spread her handkerchief over the cushion.

Holmes could be quite gentle with the opposite sex when it suited his purpose. He began his questioning in an easy, familiar manner and calming tone.

"Now, Miss Purcell," said he, "tell us what occurred on the day the Earl went missing. Exactly as you remember the events of that day, leave nothing out, even the smallest thing might be helpful in discovering the whereabouts of your employer."

"Well, sir, I only know what Mr. Jessup told us, sir. I'm never above stairs unless I'm called upon to help the house maids when there are extra guests. Mr. Jessup came down and asked us to search the kitchens, scullery, pantries, and storerooms. We did so and found no sign of his Lordship."

"And there was nothing else," Holmes pressed gently.

Miss Purcell shook her head. "No, sir."

"Was there nothing that caught your attention or that seemed odd or out of place?" He looked at her expectantly.

She thought a moment, pursed her lips, and looked to the door as if seeking the approval of Jessup.

"There was one thing, sir," she began — then stopped and looked down at her shoes.

Holmes was sitting at attention now. "Pray continue, Miss Purcell."

Her cheeks flushed. "Oh, sir, I shouldn't. You'll think it silly and Mr. Jessup …"

"Never mind, Mr. Jessup," Holmes said. "Tell me what it is that you found so unusual as to retain in your memory."

"Very well, sir," she said. "After we searched for his Lordship, I brought the breakfast dishes into the scullery to wash them. When I reached under the sink for my bucket of soap and my pail of rags and brushes, they were nowhere to be found. I was quite cross as I imagined someone was playing tricks on me, as I'm the youngest of the inside servants and the newest here as well. No one in the kitchen claimed to know anything about it and I was forced to hunt around for what I needed to do a proper job. I got behind in my work and Cook reprimanded me quite sharpish. I tried to tell her what had happened, but she would hear none of it. Later, Mrs. Porter came in and scolded me for leaving my buckets and rags in the lower passage of the servants' hall, which I hadn't done."

Holmes was practically vibrating with excitement, though I didn't see how this revelation of what was obviously a servants' prank, most likely to haze the girl or to get back at her for some inconsequential slight real or imagined, would be of any help to us.

"Was the culprit discovered?" Holmes asked. "Did anyone admit to the deed?"

"No, sir," she said.

"Has your equipment been tampered with since or any other prank played upon you?"

"No, sir, nothing of the kind."

"Thank you, Miss Purcell. You may go. You've been most helpful. Please ask Mr. Gladney to come in."

Emily Purcell, looking much relieved, stood, removed her handkerchief from the cushion, curtsied, and slipped quickly out the door. A moment later, the groom, Jim Gladney, cap in hand, stepped into the sitting room. He was a tall, lanky lad with shrewd eyes that belied his young age. He had a shock of sandy hair with a forelock that fell across his face no matter how many times he brushed it aside.

Holmes waved him in and bid him sit. He, too, spread his handkerchief on the cushion before taking his seat.

"Mr. Gladney," Holmes said. "I am well aware of the servants' code in great houses such as this. The family's business is not to be discussed with strangers. I also understand that you fear for your position should you reveal something that either incriminates you or is taken for disloyalty. However, your master and your mistress are in great danger, as is the Earl, should he still be alive. If you know something that could help me, and you fail to divulge it, you will bring disaster upon this house."

Holmes delivered this speech in the sternest possible voice while fixing the young groom with an unrelenting stare. I could only imagine that frustration had finally got the better of my friend for he had hardly been as severe with the other servants. Despite Holmes's forcefulness, I fully expected the young man to repeat what his fellow servants had told us.

"Now, Mr. Gladney," Holmes continued, "will you tell us what you know of the Earl's disappearance and why you withheld this knowledge from Lord Silverpin and lied to the police?"

The boy had gone quite pale. He extricated himself from Holmes's gaze with difficulty. I observed a slight tremor in his fingers as he turned his cap around and around in his hands. After a long pause, he looked up, the signs of an internal struggle etched upon his features.

"How did you know, Mr. Holmes?"

"I saw you yesterday," Holmes replied in a much milder tone. "You were engaged in what I can only say appeared to be an animated dispute with Mr. Staunton. Both of you displayed a considerable amount of agitation."

Holmes now had the groom's full attention, as well as mine.

"There was no other serious trouble on the estate. This I discovered when I spoke to the stable boys last night when, I suspect, you were on another of your amorous forays."

Jim Gladney's flushed cheeks confirmed Holmes's deduction.

"Mr. Staunton is your superior. What could have induced you to remonstrate with him in such a way that might very well result in your dismissal?"

"What indeed?" I remarked.

"I also learned from the stable boys that you and Mr. Staunton are as thick as thieves. They cannot recall a single harsh word ever exchanged between you. So, I asked myself, what brought about this abrupt change in character. There might be any number of explanations, but the one that seems most likely under the circumstances is the arrival of myself and Dr. Watson at Highmount House for the purpose of discovering the whereabouts of the Earl. How am I doing, Mr. Gladney?"

Jim Gladney hung his head and looked sideways at Holmes with what I can only describe as an utterly contrite expression.

"You are right about that, Mr. Holmes," said the groom. "I didn't want to be the cause of trouble for Mr. Staunton for until recently he's been better to me than my own dad."

"How has Mr. Staunton changed?" I asked.

"I can't rightly say, sir. Just that he's not himself, if you know what I mean. He's come over all queer somehow. Sometimes, I feel he's not the same man."

"When did you first notice this change in demeanor?"

"A few weeks before the Earl went missing, I reckon."

"Tell us," Holmes said, "what caused your argument with Mr. Staunton?"

"I saw Mr. Staunton and the Earl drive out on the morning the police said the Earl disappeared."

Holmes and I stared at the young man in disbelief for a few seconds. Then Holmes collected himself sufficiently to continue questioning the lad.

"Quite early that morning, sir, oh, it must have been around four o'clock. I know the hour as I had to get back afore anyone discovered I'd been out and about. I saw Mr. Staunton set off with his Lordship for the train station with them crates bound for London. At least I thought it was the Earl, the way he was dressed and all. It was a full moon so I could see tolerable well."

"Why do you believe now that it wasn't the Earl you saw?"

"Because, sir, the Earl would not have traveled with Mr. Staunton in the wagon. He'd have Mr. Staunton bring him to the station later in the carriage."

"Did you ask Mr. Staunton about this?"

"Yes, sir."

"How did he explain it?"

"He said he was takin' the crates to the station as instructed."

"And the person with him?"

"He said it was a man needin' a ride to another village and I shouldn't say nothin' about it as we could both lose our positions and be dismissed without letters. But now the papers are sayin' the Earl did go to London, that he was seen there."

"Why did you not tell this to the police?"

"I never saw a policeman. Mr. Staunton spoke for all us under him. And, anyhow, Mr. Staunton said the police would try and trick us into sayin' something incrim, incrim …"

"Incriminating," Holmes prompted.

"Yeah, that we done something wrong, and that you would do the same."

"You could have gone to the police independently."

"No, sir. I had been in the village during the night with a girl and us alone without a chaperone. Well, if that word had got 'round I would have lost my position and ruined the young lady's reputation. And anyway, Mr. Staunton said if the police got wind of our doin's, they would lay the blame on him because he was easy at hand, and they just might take me along as an accomplice as they wouldn't believe I was just out for a stroll on a bone-chillin' night in November. At the very least they'd suspect me of bein' up to no good. It would be a stain on me, sir, and her people not yet keen on me."

"I understand your concerns, Mr. Gladney," Holmes said. "At first you saw no harm in keeping quiet because you trusted Mr. Staunton, but as time passed your concerns grew."

"Yes, sir."

"You've done well in confiding in us, young man. And we will do well by you; I give you my word. But you must help us in this matter in every way you can, or else matters may proceed as you fear." Holmes stood and offered his hand to the groom. After a moment of surprise, Jim Gladney gripped Holmes's hand and shook it heartily as a look of relief swept over his features.

"I will, Mr. Holmes. Call upon me whenever you need me and tell me what I must do."

Holmes returned to his chair. "The other man in the wagon, what did he look like? Can you describe him? Take your time. Was there anything about him that was striking?"

"He was bundled up like a sausage. I couldn't see much of his face for his muffler covered half of it and his hat was pulled down tight."

"How can you be sure it wasn't the Earl? You were quite some distance away, up by the chapel?"

Jim Gladney gave a start. "It's as if you were there watchin' me yourself, Mr. Holmes. That's where I was all right. But I'll stick to it that it couldn't have been the Earl because he'd never travel in that wagon. He wanted his comfort and his privacy."

"Thank you, Mr. Gladney," said Holmes. "Before you go, might I ask you one more question?"

"Of course, sir,"

"Do you know what happened to the gentleman who preceded Mr. Jessup?"

The relief which young Jim had recently experienced fled him in an instant. He clutched at his cap and his whole body tensed as an expression of distress flashed across his face.

"Now, now, Mr. Gladney," Holmes said. "You've come this far. You will not stick now, will you?"

Jim Gladney swallowed, then sighed shakily. "That would be Mr. Arthur, sir. He was killed defendin' the house durin' a break in."

"What?" I gasped.

"I expected as much," said Holmes. "Now, Mr. Gladney, one last question. Where is Mr. Staunton? I've been after him all day, and no one has seen him. It is important that I speak with him as he appears to be the last person to see the Earl."

"I can't say, Mr. Holmes," said Jim Gladney. "We seen him this mornin' first thing, when he gave us our instructions. But, we've not seen hide nor hair of him since."

Chapter Eight

That night, we dined alone in our rooms. I ate heartily after such an exhausting day. Holmes, deep in thought, pushed his meal away. He rose, went to the window, drew the heavy curtains aside, and looked out into the night. As city dwellers, we were accustomed to the constant clamor of humanity outside our walls. Here in the heart of Hampshire, I found the deep silence of the countryside unnerving. Holmes had said nothing more about the watchers. Did they still lurk out there in the dark? My senses were on high alert, a remnant of my military service in Afghanistan. I recalled the battle of Maiwand when we waited through the night in an agony of anticipation and dread for the attack we knew must come, not knowing when the enemy would strike or the devastating odds we would face.

"The wind is picking up," said Holmes as he turned away from the window.

"Yes," I agreed as I inclined an ear to the glass. The wind buffeting the house caused the casements to creak and undoubtedly was the source of the draught chilling my ankles. With the advent of the wind the temperature in our rooms had plummeted. Holmes felt it too, for I saw a shiver pass through him before he placed another log upon the low-burning fire.

"Coal is more reliable," he muttered as he held his hands close to the hearth.

I found the constant fretting of the wind unsettling. Rising, I closed the gap in the curtains, moved our chairs closer to the fire, and filled two glasses with port, a small bulwark against the anxiety that had once again beset me.

"In the next day or so, I will be ready to report our progress to his Lordship," Holmes said.

"I cannot see that we've made any progress in discovering the whereabouts of the Earl."

"Pish posh, old man, I need only a few more pieces of this puzzle and the picture will become clear."

Before I could reply, he pressed on, pacing to and fro before the fire.

"Why did the Silverpins decide to act now?" said he, brandishing his pipe. "Something has happened. It might have been the murder of Sir Roger. But I think not. It is more likely something of which we are unaware. Whatever that event may be, it impelled them to action; but that is a puzzle for the morrow."

"Let us get back to the business of today," I said. "You obviously discovered much during your nighttime foray. Will you not tell me more of what you have learned?"

"Quite right, old friend, I have gotten ahead of myself," said he. He knocked his pipe on the grate before returning to his chair, then re-packed the bowl, struck a match, and lit the strong black shag he favored.

"Deposit our tray on the hall table if you will. There's a good fellow. That way we shan't be disturbed by the maid."

I did as he requested, then poked at the fire before settling again in my chair. I filled my pipe while Holmes further apprised me of his previous night's discoveries.

"Do you recall when we were in the Earl's study? I was examining the bookcases near the vault?"

"Indeed, I do. You acted most peculiarly."

"I was looking for a hidden door. I was on the point of despair when it dawned on me where that door must be."

"How the devil did you know to look for a hidden door at all?"

"Because I knew it must be there. In a building of such venerable age, it would be surprising if there were not. I entered the vault and discovered that the wall of shelves at the back opens onto a stair that leads to an underground chamber, and from that chamber proceeds a tunnel that runs all the way to the chapel."

"Good lord! The chapel is a quarter mile or more away. One can't even see it from the house."

"That, of course, is entirely the point!" Holmes exclaimed. "One might call it a priests' hole, but the Earls of Convarran constructed these secret passages long before Henry's reign. Heaven knows for what purpose, though I suspect they were a means of escape should the castle come under siege. Nevertheless, through this tunnel, the Earl removed himself from the house without being seen — or how someone removed him. I am certain of it. And it was near the chapel, was it not, that Jim Gladney saw Staunton and the person he at first took to be the Earl?"

"Why should the Earl wish to come and go in secret?"

Holmes chuckled. "I believe his objective was to conceal his collection. That is, his actual collection — not what we were shown in the study. The genuine items were brought in secretly through the tunnel."

"If the Earl were taken from the house by these blackguards, how did they know of the tunnel? Surely, they must have had a confederate inside Highmount."

"So, it would seem."

"The Silverpins must know of these passages. Yet they said nothing."

"Without a doubt they know of them," said Holmes.

"What is down there? Anything that can help us find the Earl?"

"A room filled with gold, jewels, and precious objects. A collection of antiquities that is quite breathtaking. What is it these people are after, Watson, to leave such priceless treasures untouched? And blood, Watson. I found what I believe to be traces of blood."

"Then the Earl was assaulted and possibly fought back against his attackers, no doubt the very same scoundrels who assaulted you!" I surmised.

"It is tempting to assume so, and it might very well be the Earl's blood, but it might also be someone else's. In any case, someone did their best to sponge away the stains. It has to be someone aware of the routines of the house, and more importantly someone who knew where Miss Purcell worked and that they would find there the tools needed to do the job."

"Her missing bucket and rags."

"Exactly."

"But why did they not replace them where they found them?"

"Perhaps they could not."

"I still say this whole affair must have something to do with what happened in Egypt. But Holmes, I'm dashed if I can see how all the pieces fit together. If only we knew what had transpired during that expedition."

"As it happens, I do know what happened at Dahshoor." Holmes reached into the pocket of his dressing gown and held up the Earl's personal journal.

"Of course!" I exclaimed.

"It is extensive," said Holmes. "The Earl was a copious if erratic recorder of all that he did and thought. I read quite a bit while you slept."

"Is there any clue as to who might have abducted him?"

"In good time, Watson, all in good time. Listen to this entry."

He read thusly…

"Monday, 2 September, 1889

Our first day in the field and the week that followed were uneventful. We hired laborers, set up camp, surveyed the site, and made plans on how best to proceed. The pyramid of Amenemhat III is our object, as this is the pyramid that Emm claims holds a great treasure, if only we can discover a way into the underground passages and reach the pharaoh's burial chamber. If they've been filled with rubble, it will be the devil's own work to clear them. If collapse has destroyed them, I fear we will have wasted our time and resources as we are not equipped for such a major undertaking at this time as would be required to open and fortify the substructure."

Holmes continued, "And this, a week later …

"Tuesday, 10 September, 1889

There is unrest among the laborers. The men do their work but watch us with furtive glances and much muttering among themselves. We all speak a smattering of Arabic, with Neferuptah and Matheson the most fluent. Neferuptah remains our only reliable means of communicating with the fellahin, as they are her people. I have asked her to discover what is troubling them. The men are reluctant to speak, even to one of their own, about anything other than matters concerning their daily work. Her family is an ancient and respected one claiming lineage from the God-Kings. Thus, it is my hope that she will be able to draw them out. From the little I can glean from their chattering it seems that, among the locals, this place has an evil reputation.

"And then, two days later …

"Thursday, 12 September, 1889

The news that Neferuptah brings is troubling. The Black Pyramid, as it has come to be known, is believed to be a source of evil. The fact that the pyramid appears to be rotting from the inside confirms in the minds of the fellahin that a sinister influence, an ancient evil, if you will, lies buried beneath it, and that this presence remains active and potent. All nonsense of course, but there is no reasoning with these people."

Suddenly, without warning, a log exploded spewing a shower of sparks upon the carpet. Startled, my heart pounding, I leapt up and stamped upon the embers. Holmes, a look of surprise on his face, gripped the arms of his chair. We then sat for some moments in silence. It wasn't until we had each taken another glass of port that Holmes continued reading, and even then, I thought I detected a slight quaver in his voice.

"This entry was written a fortnight hence," said he as he found his place among the pages.

"Thursday, 26 September, 1889

After much clearing away and sifting of debris, we have begun examining the pyramid's base in search of concealed entrances to the substructure. As a result, our troubles have increased alarmingly. At first, supplies and equipment were discovered missing, forcing us to travel to Cairo to replace the stolen items. Finding us undeterred in our work, the harassment has escalated to sabotage, in one instance nearly resulting in Matheson's death. Last night, however, was the last straw. Trumbull was attacked in his tent while he slept. His cries woke us, but if there was an intruder, he had fled into the night. Trumbull remembers little other than waking from night terrors and seeing a figure that he could only describe as a "black pharaoh" of evil countenance. I do not believe our laborers are responsible, but I cannot be sure. With each new incident, they jabber about curses. Some have already gone, and the rest are on the point of bolting.

Holmes coughed, cleared his throat, and coughed again. "I'm getting a bit dry, old man, would you kindly fetch me a glass of water."

I did as he requested and waited in fervent anticipation as he slowly sipped the water allowing it to lubricate his throat.

"And this," he said at last, "two days later ...

"Saturday, 28 September, 1889

As if our present troubles are not serious enough. Emm has been acting most peculiarly and looking even more cadaverous than usual. His flesh is all of a deathly pallor and his eyes appear bruised and are sunk into his skull. He eats almost nothing yet secretes a malodorous perspiration and a foul breath. He has taken to rambling about in the night despite our warnings that he is in danger of being attacked. We have no idea where he goes as there is nothing but desert surrounding us. Matheson has attempted to follow him but without success. Yet any attempt to draw him out is met with what I can only describe as a sly evasiveness. Pressing him only draws his ire. Such is Neferuptah's distress and her conviction that we should leave this place in all haste that she came to me and told me of an undiscovered tomb filled with riches in the Valley of the Kings. The knowledge of this tomb has been in her family for generations, and they are, she claims, the guardians of this knowledge. I can only guess at the depth of her terror that has caused her to share this secret. She has shown me proof of its existence. As in all things, my faith and trust in her is unshakable as she has never shown me anything but the most steadfast loyalty.

"And this, written a few days before they departed Egypt …

"Wednesday, 2 October, 1889

Neferuptah came to me this morning with whispers overheard from the few fellahin who are still with us. They are with us only because she has told them that we intend to leave and has set them to packing our remaining property. Our reis, a man she knows personally, told her that Emm, during his nighttime excursions, had found a passage into a burial chamber. That he told no one of his discovery is both appalling and infuriating. It is also whispered that he brought out objects from the chamber. When confronted, he denied the accusation, but when he realized we were determined to investigate further, he threatened our lives. Matheson had to restrain him so we could search his bags. He howled and cursed like a madman all the while. What our reis said is true: Hidden away in a secret compartment in one of his cases were a strange papyrus and an oddly shaped stone. I have no idea what these objects are or why he sought to conceal them as they appear to have no great value.

"And here, Watson, attend to this undated entry. I believe we are getting to the heart of the matter.

"It was decided among Matheson, Trumbull, and myself that the punishment for Emm's deceit, and perhaps for the treacherous complicity of which we are yet unaware, will be, once we reach Cairo, to abandon him in the Old City without resources and return to England without him. I confiscated the objects Emm had stolen. It is my intention to turn them over to the Service des Antiquities upon our arrival in Cairo."

Holmes paused in his recitation and cocked his head toward the door. He held a finger to his lips, slipped from his chair and glided soundlessly across the room. Without warning he threw open the door and thrust his head into the hall. I jumped to my feet and hurried to his side. We peered right and left. The hall was empty.

"You heard something?" I asked.

Holmes nodded.

"Surely, it was the maid passing."

"If it was," Holmes inclined his head to the hall table, "she failed to remove our dishes."

Holmes glanced once more up and down the hall before we returned to the fire, and he read the last entry in the journal penned on the day the Earl returned to England.

"As for myself, my relief is great. The truth is that had we found the Black Pyramid packed with gold, even then I would not have stayed. Day after day, I dragged myself through narrow, low-ceilinged passageways searching for a way into the pharaoh's burial chamber. My lungs labored for every breath until I could only gasp for air as I struggled. After each unsuccessful attempt to discover a way into the chamber, I emerged covered in a vile black dust. Even now, thousands upon thousands of miles away, I feel the taint of the place upon my person, as much from the Black Pyramid itself as from those objects taken from it."

"Good, lord, Holmes, it is Emm! It must be. He's made his way back from Cairo and is taking revenge on his former compatriots."

"I'm inclined to agree. However, there is more. I fear we are in deep and murky waters."

A sharp look from Holmes followed by a glance at the door halted our conversation. I heard voices and the rattle of dishes followed by a staccato rapping on the door.

"Come," said Holmes.

At Holmes's command, a footman entered. "Begging your pardon, sir, a telegram has just arrived for you."

He handed the telegram to Holmes and with a curt bow departed.

"It must be urgent," I said, "for the station master to send a boy out at this hour."

"Indeed," said Holmes. "It is from Lestrade." He opened the telegram, read it, and gave a low whistle.

"What does he say? Has he news about the Earl?"

"Disaster!" exclaimed Holmes. "Lestrade has been removed from the case and replaced by an Inspector Aloysius Crowe."

"What does it mean?" I asked. "Why would the Yard replace Lestrade? You have said yourself that he is one of their best."

"I don't know, Watson. This Crowe is not known to me. Who and what he is and whether he is friend or foe we will have to discover."

Chapter Nine

The next morning, after we had breakfasted and returned to our rooms a footman appeared and delivered to Holmes a packet of his post and two telegrams. I have never known Sherlock Holmes to be away from Baker Street for any length of time without setting up a communications network. Our sojourn with the Silverpins was no different; the pile of post on our table grew by the hour. Indeed, such a quantity of information had arrived that Holmes had declared this to be a day of analysis and thought. And though I was fairly bursting with questions, I sank into my easy chair and put my feet up to toast upon the fender leaving my friend to his correspondence and to ponder and, I dared to hope, unravel this unfathomable and outré case.

Holmes opened the first telegram, scanned it, and gave a low whistle.

"As it happens, this telegram is from Inspector Crowe. He says he has received a report from the British Museum regarding the scarabs and will share it with us. Apparently, the primary conclusion is that they are not of this Earth."

"Not of this Earth! Good lord, what do they mean by that?"

"For heaven's sake, man, there is nothing unusual in that. Debris has been falling to Earth from space for millennia. Chladni identified the first meteoric rock in 1794. That someone in ancient Egypt came across some fragments of a similar material and used it to create these scarabs is hardly surprising."

Holmes puffed on his pipe, producing a cloud of smoke that scented the air with its pungent aroma.   .

"Poor Lestrade," said I, changing the subject in the hope of avoiding one of my friend's scholarly lectures. "I hope nothing ill has befallen him."

Holmes cocked his head to one side at this and let out another great exhalation of smoke. "It is unlikely that Lestrade has been replaced for incompetence if that is what you're imagining. The Yard is besieged on all sides of late. There is great unrest in the East End, particularly in Whitechapel, due to a growing discontent with the influx of Jewish immigrants from the Continent and the ensuing lack of employment which is driving up crime of all kinds. If Lestrade is to concentrate his efforts solely in Whitechapel without other distractions, it is all for the better."

"Have you found anything out about this Crowe fellow?"

"Nothing. I have so far been unable to turn up anything significant about him."

"Lestrade must be beside himself."

"Perhaps," said Holmes. "On the other hand, he may be quite relieved. He has more than enough on his plate, particularly with these recent murders. It is interesting — they appear random, and yet a pattern of sorts is emerging that conceals a hidden order: similar victims, seemingly without motive, violent in the extreme, and with little or no evidence left behind."

"A lunatic, at the source, surely."

Holmes removed the pipe from his mouth and pointed the stem at me. "Not a madman in the sense you are thinking of, old fellow. These individuals are insane, yes, but not the raving lunatics one finds in Bethlehem Asylum. Just the opposite, in fact. They are cold, calculating, exceedingly clever, intelligent, and confident to the point of arrogance."

"I shall take your word for it," I said. "At any rate, I would like to meet this Crowe fellow and get the measure of him."

"He has banned us from the Yard except by appointment."

"Banned!" I cried, bridling at the word.

"Calm yourself, old man," said Holmes with a chuckle. "You will have your opportunity anon. We will make an appointment and consult with Inspector Crowe when we return to London."

"You have a second telegram there. Who is that from?"

Holmes picked up the telegram from the table and opened it. "Ah," he said, "it is a communication from my brother."

"What does he say?"

"He requests an audience with us at his club."

"Will you see him?"

"Eventually. We have too many other engagements. Mycroft will have to wait."

As Holmes commenced perusing his post, there was yet another knock at our door.

"Come," called Holmes.

A young boy entered. A houseboy, I presumed, by the look of him, about the age of our Billy. He held out his tray on which lay a letter.

"This is just come for you in the post, sir."

Holmes took the letter and fished a farthing from his waistcoat pocket and passed it to the boy.

"Thank you, sir!" said the lad, and he dashed out the door clutching his prize.

Holmes held up the letter and examined it in the light. "If I am not mistaken, this is a message from Porlock."

He slit open the envelope with his pocketknife and withdrew a single sheet of paper. As he read, his brow furrowed, and his already thin lips formed a tight, grim line.

"Whatever is it, old man?" I asked. "Who is this Porlock and what does he say?"

Holmes turned the paper so that I could see a single line scrawled on its surface. Squinting, I tried to make out what was written. "I cannot make it out," I said.

"The message reads: 'We are at war!' "

"What the devil is that supposed to mean?"

Holmes crushed the paper into a ball and tossed it into the fire where it was consumed in an instant.

"Porlock is a minion of Professor Moriarty. This Porlock, for reasons I have been unable to discover, upon the rare occasion, communicates with me in code or riddles concerning the activities of his master. Have I not mentioned Moriarty?"

"You have. I recall you speaking of him some time ago."

"Allow me to refresh your memory. I shall spare you a recitation of his sordid history. Suffice it to say the man is a criminal genius; a Napoleon of crime, if you will. There is nothing of a nefarious or criminal nature that happens in London of which Professor Moriarty is not aware or that is beyond his grasp."

"But why does this Porlock speak of war? And what has it to do with our case?"

"It may have nothing to do with it or everything. That is what I must discover."

"Can the police not lay their hands upon this Moriarty or this Porlock and question them?"

"Would that they could, Watson. Would that they could. The villain is so cunning and elusive that he has never been seen. Why, he could be anyone with whom we've crossed paths of late, as could Porlock, and we none the wiser. If Moriarty's influence is at work in this matter, then it takes on an even more sinister aspect."

My spirit sank. "What will you do?" I asked in growing concern. Every day it seemed brought some new and disturbing complication to burden my friend and further tax his extraordinary faculties.

"I must think," he replied. "You must let me think."

The great detective then settled himself in his armchair with his black shag close at hand and turned his gaze away from me and towards the flames in the hearth. Within moments, that dreamy, far-off look came into his eyes, and I knew that he would remain so, unmoving and uncommunicative, for the rest of the day, and even into the night, as his great mind turned over and analyzed every aspect of the information he had gathered.

Chapter Ten

The next morning, drawn by the aroma of coffee and sausages, we went down to breakfast and found Lord Silverpin pacing the dining room in great agitation. As we entered, he spun around to face us.

"Some further deviltry has occurred, Mr. Holmes, though we confess, we do not know what to make of it."

Lady Vivienne, seated at the table, appeared to be in a state of extreme distress. I recognized the signs of nervous strain: a furrowed brow, tightness about the mouth, a rigid posture, and staring eyes. I further observed she held in her hands a napkin that she twisted and untwisted in a most violent fashion.

A slug of adrenaline shot threw me as I imagined Lord Silverpin had discovered the theft of the Earl's journal from his bedchamber.

"Calm yourself, Lord Silverpin," Holmes said. "Come, sit, and tell me what has happened."

Holmes's eyes were alight with eagerness. So confident was he that he took Lord Silverpin by the arm — a shocking breach of etiquette — and guided him to the table where they sat down next to one another, so close their knees almost touched.

"We have received a message," Lord Silverpin said as he passed Holmes the letter clutched in his hand.

"A message from your father," Holmes remarked as he examined the paper and the envelope that contained it.

My fears allayed for the moment; I took a seat near Lady Vivienne.

"Cream paper of good quality." Holmes held the letter up to the light pouring through the dining room window. "Yet it lacks a watermark. Can't be traced. Hand-written in India ink with a broad stub dip pen. No blots. Someone who does a good bit of writing. A man's hand surely." He sniffed the paper and his nose wrinkled. "An odd scent," he murmured to himself. He set the letter on the table and took up the envelope. "Postmarked yesterday in London."

Holmes set the envelope aside and took up the letter. He read thusly:

"My dearest children, I beg your pardon and ask your forgiveness for the worry and upset that, after reading the papers, I am sure I have caused you. I was called away upon a matter of the utmost urgency; secrecy was demanded. In the events that followed, we encountered some trouble, and I was unavoidably detained and unable to communicate with you. All is well now, and I am writing to ask you to reschedule the program at the Egyptian Hall. I have communicated with Matheson and he is agreeable. I will make my appearance during the performance and after, I will join you and all will be explained."

"Surely, that is good news," I said. "Except …"

"If this message is from the Earl," said Holmes, "then it is indeed good news, except that this letter gives credence to the Earl's disappearance as a publicity stunt. However, there is reason to doubt its provenance."

Holmes set the letter on the table before Lord Silverpin and Lady Vivienne. "Is this your father's handwriting?"

Lord Silverpin took up the letter and they examined it closely. He looked at his sister and she nodded.

"It appears to be," said he.

"I take it you have not yet communicated this to the police?" asked Holmes.

"No," said Lord Silverpin. "There has not been time and we …"

"Say nothing to the police," said Holmes. "I will take it up with Inspector Crowe when we return to London."

"Who is Inspector Crowe?" asked Lady Vivienne.

"I've had a message from Inspector Lestrade," Holmes explained. "He has been removed from your case and Inspector Aloysius Crowe has been installed in his place. At the moment, we know nothing else. However, under the circumstances, it is prudent to wait until we can meet and get the measure of the man."

"Of course, just as you say, Mr. Holmes," said Lord Silverpin.

"It is our dearest hope that this message is from our father, but we fear it is not," said Lady Vivienne. "Surely, if this communication is truly from him, he would have more to say to us than just these few vague words and would provide a way for us to communicate with him. There is no return address. If our father is in London, why is he not at our Mayfair residence?"

"Perhaps the Earl is traveling so a reply would not reach him," I offered.

Before I could say more, Holmes responded, "It is far more likely that this message comes from your father's abductors and is an attempt to lure you away from Highmount House for the purpose of gaining access in your absence or because they wish to entrap you. But, you say you believe the handwriting is his."

"We do," said Lady Vivienne.

"If that is so, then it is undoubtedly coerced. Perhaps we can verify your belief by comparing the handwriting in the letter to that in your father's private journal." Holmes removed the volume from his pocket and set it on the table before the astonished faces of the Silverpins.

"How ..." Lord Silverpin began.

"You know a great deal more about this business than you have told us," Holmes said sternly. "That much I have ascertained. If you will not be honest with me in all things, I cannot continue in your employ. In any case, will you not give these people what they want, and with all haste? Certainly, no antiquity is more valuable than your father's life."

At Holmes's words, Lord Silverpin paled. The cup from which Lady Vivienne sipped her coffee slipped from her fingers and clattered into its saucer. The servant Neferuptah, who must have been listening at the door, burst into the room.

"You must not!" she cried.

"Well, well," said Holmes with a satisfied smile. He withdrew from his coat pocket the photograph he'd shown me earlier and laid it upon the table. "I wondered when we'd be hearing from your mother."

The look of utter shock upon the Silverpins' faces mirrored my own.

"If you know this, Mr. Holmes, then you must know all," declared Lady Vivienne.

"I know a great deal, but not all," said Holmes. He tapped the Earl's journal. "I took the liberty of searching your room, Lord Silverpin, and found the journal in your escritoire. From it, I learned the true account of what occurred in Egypt."

Lord Silverpin struggled to control the emotions warring across his countenance. At last, with an effort, he spoke. "That was indeed a liberty, Mr. Holmes. But under the circumstances, I suppose we can hardly blame you."

"You concealed the very thing that has the power to guide us to the heart of this matter," said Holmes. "Why?"

"On the very day that we engaged you, these people somehow learned of our efforts," Lord Silverpin admitted.

Holmes interjected. "You had some communication from the kidnappers?"

"We did."

"Aha! Watson, I told you so." Holmes flung himself from his chair and began to pace around the room. "You will tell me all. All. Your very lives may depend upon it."

To my surprise, he delivered these statements not in the stern manner as before, but in a gentle, yet emphatic tone.

Perhaps he had come to the conclusion, as had I, that the Silverpins' deceit was not malicious, but born of fear and a sense of helplessness.

"We will tell you all we know and what we suspect, Mr. Holmes," said Lord Silverpin. "But we fear you will think us fools at best, or worse, quite mad."

"Let me be the judge of that."

"Very well," Lord Silverpin began. "On the very day we returned home after consulting you, we received an anonymous message about our father. We were to give no other information of any kind to the authorities on pain of his death. We were to wait for a further communication."

"These scoundrels were alerted immediately upon your engaging me. Who knew you were coming to see me?" Holmes asked.

"Your brother, of course. We acted upon his recommendation that very day."

"I can assure you, my brother is innocent of any treachery," Holmes said. "Who else?"

"The only other person who knew of our visit to you …" Lord Silverpin ceased speaking mid-sentence as the answer struck him.

"Your man, Staunton," Holmes said quietly.

"We cannot believe it!" cried Lady Vivienne.

"You must," said Holmes and he repeated to them what Jim Gladney had told us.

"We are stunned," said Lord Silverpin.

I had no doubt of it by the look of shock upon their faces.

"Staunton grew up in this house. His family has served us for generations."

"This spy in your house must be removed with all haste," declared Holmes.

Lord Silverpin leapt to his feet and moved toward the bell pull. "We shall have it out with him this very moment!"

"No," said Holmes. "You must do exactly as I say. Staunton must have no warning our net is closing around him."

"Very well," said Lord Silverpin. "We are in your hands, Mr. Holmes."

Lady Vivienne nodded her assent.

"In regard to the other matter, the police would not have believed us," said Lord Silverpin. "And, the knowledge would not have helped them find our father. In your case, Mr. Holmes, we wanted to get the measure of you first. If during your visit to Highmount House, we felt we could trust you, we intended to confide in you despite your brother advising against it."

The look of utter surprise that appeared upon Holmes's face lasted only a second before he composed himself. "Did he now? I shall have to have a word with him."

I did not know the tenor of Holmes's relationship with his brother. But for him to recommend Holmes's services while suggesting subterfuge was remarkable indeed. I wondered what my friend's response to such an insult would be.

During these revelations, Neferuptah, who I now knew to be Lord Silverpin's and Lady Vivienne's mother, sat silently beside her children, taking in all that was said. Before continuing, Holmes glanced at her, and she steadily returned his gaze.

"Let us begin," said Holmes, returning his attention to Lord Silverpin and Lady Vivienne. "Before I reveal what I have inferred from the facts I have gathered, pray, tell me, what is in your possession that these people want so badly. It is obvious that whatever your father confiscated from Emm in Egypt was not returned to the Service des Antiquities. He kept them and managed to bring them back to England with no one the wiser. That implies the objects must be quite small. It is also singular that your father did not describe these objects in his journal. Were Matheson and Trumbull aware that he brought them here?"

"No," said Lord Silverpin. "Sir Roger and Mr. Matheson were not aware. We ourselves, did not know of the existence of these objects until the Earl began acting strangely. Indeed, it was our mother who discovered the source of our father's strange behavior. It was the papyrus and stone he had taken from Professor Emm."

"In what way had your father's behavior changed from what you have already described?"

This time, it was Neferuptah who spoke.

"He slept even more infrequently than before. Sometimes it seemed that he slept not at all. He shut himself up in his study for hours on end and would not respond to any summons. He had a haunted look about him and he seemed constantly on edge, his nerves were quite frayed. Unlocking the secrets of the papyrus and the stone became his obsession. They consumed him. He also became quite fearful of thieves and of the house being burgled."

"That fear — of the watchers that lurked outside — being the reason for the Egyptian wards placed near every door and window in this house that are meant to deter thieves and protect the faithful," said Holmes. He removed the vault key from his pocket and laid it atop the Earl's journal. Lord Silverpin stared at the key and then at Holmes. For a long moment, his expression was unreadable. I reckoned he had just acquired a greater appreciation of Holmes's extraordinary skills.

"Yes," Lord Silverpin admitted. "That is correct. You continue to amaze us, Mr. Holmes. It seems we are an open book to you."

"And now, Madam," said Holmes focusing his attention on Neferuptah. "Your involvement in this matter is vast. I have noted your presence in the background of every photograph of the Earl's digs and you feature prominently in his private journal. It takes no great intellect to deduce that you are much more than a nursemaid — a great deal more I should think. Come now, you cannot remain in the shadows forever. It is time for you to explain yourself."

Chapter Eleven

At this admonishment from Holmes, Neferuptah bridled and said in an imperious voice, "Do not judge what you do not understand, Mr. Holmes."

"Then, pray, enlighten us, Madam."

"The Countess was a sickly woman. Egypt did not agree with her, but she would not be separated from her husband. She could not produce children. Two had already perished before they drew breath. So, the Earl …" She trailed off.

"The Earl …?" Holmes prompted her.

"The Countess claimed our children as her own," Neferuptah said angrily. "She saw the babies were strong and quick. She saw what might be. A son and heir; a daughter desirable to wealthy and powerful men." Neferuptah gave us a ferocious look. "That I birthed them must never be known. Never! Do you understand? That secret must be preserved."

"If the matter has no bearing upon the case, I see no reason to reveal these circumstances. You have my word. Watson?"

"Of course," I agreed.

"And now, Madam," said Holmes. "You were with the Earl and his companions at Dahshoor. We know from the Earl's diary that from the beginning, the expedition experienced increasing levels of harassment in what would seem an attempt to drive them off. And you were so distressed by the situation that, as a means of inducing him to leave, you revealed to the Earl the location of an undisturbed tomb that had been protected by your family for centuries. What could have such power as to cause you to betray such a trust?"

"An evil that if released would bring misery and suffering to all it touched, would corrupt everyone it touched," Neferuptah said.

"Does this corruption have a name?"

"It is called the Black Pharaoh, among other names. An evil man called Nophru-Ka usurped the throne of Amenemhat III and turned his pyramid — which is now known as the Black Pyramid — into a monument to the Black Pharaoh. This god, whose true name is forbidden to be spoken aloud, demanded blood sacrifices and Nophru-Ka provided them. He sacrificed thousands to please this god and to receive favor from him. For his horrific deeds, Nophru-Ka became known as the Mad Pharaoh. Eventually, the people could bear his cruelty no longer and rose up against him. The priests of the old gods of Egypt, led by the Osirans, sealed Nophru-Ka alive in a hidden chamber in the Black Pyramid. In the coming years, all mention of him and his evil god were erased from history. To this day, the place itself is believed to be cursed and has been hidden from all and avoided."

"So," said Holmes, "another mummy's curse."

"No," said Neferuptah. "The Black Pharaoh is no mummy. He … it … is not of this world. The objects the Earl took from the Professor that came from the pyramid — they are not of this world."

108

"How so?" Holmes asked. "Describe these objects. What significance have they?"

"The papyrus describes a mathematical formula," said Lord Silverpin. "I am no slouch in the subject, but it is beyond my comprehension. The stone, if it is indeed a stone, is black in color, shot through with red striations. It has the shape of a trapezeohedron, though whether natural or shaped by some other agency, we cannot say."

"The stone is a window into space, time, and other dimensions, if one knows how to use it or is used by it," Neferuptah added bitterly. "It has its own agency and cannot be manipulated against its will. The papyrus describes how to create a portal into these other dimensions."

Holmes sat back in his chair. He had been listening intently, but now a shadow of contemptuous incredulity darkened his features. Yet, I would say he struggled between incredulity and curiosity, for the idea that such a thing might be a mathematical possibility would surely attract a mind such as his, yet the sheer absurdity of the notion would repel him.

"Surely, your Lordship lends no credence to this tale," said Holmes.

The young lord's expression was unreadable, but I feared Holmes had given offense as he would countenance nothing tainted with even the merest trace of the supernatural.

"Legends are built over time, Mr. Holmes, and one often finds a grain of truth amongst the chaff," Lord Silverpin replied, his words clipped, his tone haughty.

"There are more things in heaven and earth, Holmes, than are dreamt of in your philosophy," I said. I had intended my response to be lighthearted and dispel the tension, but it drew only scorn from Holmes.

"Really, Watson, if you cannot say something sensible, then, pray, hold your tongue."

His rejoinder stung and I feared what would come next. But, while Holmes addressed the Silverpins sternly, he had blunted the barb of his irritation.

"Lord Silverpin, Lady Vivienne, I cannot in good conscience continue with a case in which the client believes the malefactor to be supernatural. What would be the point?"

"Mr. Holmes, we do not ask you to believe this legend," said Lady Vivienne. "All we ask is that you discover the whereabouts of our father. We do not believe any aspect of *his* disappearance is supernatural."

As she spoke, Lord Silverpin's hands tighten on the arms of his chair, and I saw challenge rising in the young Lord's eyes.

"What was once called magic is now called science. Do you not agree, Mr. Holmes?"

"You have said so yourself, Holmes, on more than one occasion," I took pleasure in reminding him.

"Quite so," said Holmes in a more affable tone. "We shall speak of it no more."

I could not help but think that for a man such as Holmes whose mind is open to a universe of possibilities yet shuts like a trap at the slightest hint of otherworldliness to be the height of contradiction. Was our Lord, Jesus Christ, not otherworldly as well as human, and yet we question little about His provenance.

"I would like to see these objects," said Holmes, bringing the conversation back to the facts at hand.

"They are secured in the Temple," said Lady Vivienne.

"The Temple?" I asked. "Are you referring to the chapel?"

"No, Watson," said Holmes. "Lady Vivienne is referring to the Temple of the Osirans, located within this house. It was established here in Hampshire by Lord Silverpin and Lady Vivienne when they broke from the Hermetic Order of the Golden Dawn in London."

Lord Silverpin started forward in his chair. "You are very well-informed, sir. How you came by your knowledge, I cannot fathom. We are a secret order, our members known only to the initiated."

Lady Vivienne placed her hand over her brother's hand. "You astound us, sir," she said. "Your reputation is surely warranted if you have been able to discover this alliance."

"It is my business to know what others do not know," said Holmes. "But tell me if you will, what precipitated your break from that organization?"

"The Golden Dawn's reputation was tainted by the depravity of one of its members. He was expelled with extreme prejudice for wickedness and evil practices. But there are those in the Order who continue to be influenced by him," said Lord Silverpin.

"If all that is said of him is true — and we have no reason to doubt the veracity of these reports for we have witnessed some of these things with our own eyes — then we believe he must be the wickedest man in the world," said Lady Vivienne.

"Am I correct that this individual is the notorious Professor Emm?" Holmes asked.

Lord Silverpin arched an eyebrow. "You are correct. However, at the time of these events he was not known by that name. We discovered his true identity only recently, and too late."

"I take it you mean too late to warn your father?" said Holmes.

"Yes. Unfortunately," said Lady Vivienne.

Holmes nodded. "You believe Emm had an ulterior motive when he convinced your father to mount an expedition to Dahshoor."

"Most certainly," said Lady Vivienne.

"That is why this house is being watched, and why you have suffered attacks, during one of which your previous butler was killed, and it is why I was attacked," said Holmes. "Who are they, these watchers?"

"You! Attacked!" cried Lord Silverpin. "When? How?"

"The evening I declined to dine with you."

Lady Vivienne, who had moved to sit nearer her brother, now clutched his arm. Neferuptah stood behind her children, her hands resting protectively on their shoulders.

"We suspect they are the minions of Professor Emm," said Lord Silverpin. "But we cannot be sure."

"Possibly," said Holmes. "However, if that is so, there is much that makes no sense. I think perhaps there is more than one agent working against us in this matter. I have been more inclined towards this conclusion from the time you told me of my brother's advice to you, and now even more so because of the appearance of this letter seeming to be from your father."

"Who can these watchers be?" asked Lady Vivienne.

"That is what we must discover," said Holmes. "Who, how many, and what their object is. Until we know that, we are at an extreme disadvantage. However, there is no reason we cannot use this latest development to our advantage and to our adversary's detriment."

Holmes, the Silverpins, and Neferuptah fell into deep and animated discussion, and the more that was said, the more confused I became until I found myself completely at sea.

"Holmes, what the devil are you talking about?" I blurted out, allowing my irritation its full head. Then I considered our clients and said: "Lord Silverpin, Lady Vivienne, Madame Neferuptah, I apologize for my outburst, but I am completely at a loss at what is being discussed."

Holmes laid a hand on my arm. "Steady on, old man. This is hardly an opportune moment for explanations and discussion. After we've reached London and Staunton is in custody and has been questioned about his part in the matter, we will hopefully know more and can plan our strategy accordingly. Now we must examine these objects that are purported to drive men to madness and murder."

Madame Neferuptah gave her son a warning look. Lord Silverpin closed his eyes and took in a deep breath. He then gazed steadily at Holmes.

"We are sorry, Mr. Holmes. That is not possible. The objects are in the Temple and no one other than the initiated may enter."

"Then bring these objects here," said Holmes.

"They cannot be removed," said Lord Silverpin. "They are guarded there, or rather, they are imprisoned there. To remove them would be extremely dangerous."

"Lord Silverpin …" Holmes protested.

"No!" repeated Lord Silverpin. "I am sorry. It is not possible."

Chapter Twelve

The next day, after completing our morning ablutions, Holmes and I packed our bags and made our way down to the Great Hall where we found quite an assembly preparing for our return trip to London on Lord Silverpin's private train. Holmes looked refreshed, his step light, with a gleam in his eyes. I questioned him about the source of his high spirits but could get nothing out of him.

"All in good time, Watson. All in good time."

Lord Silverpin and Lady Vivienne were ready to leave, dressed in their long coats and furs. Besides Holmes and I, the rest of our party consisted of Lord Silverpin's valet Alexander; Lady Vivienne's personal maid, Miss Stoddard; Jessup; Staunton; Jim Gladney; and a maid of all work. Holmes's elevated mood informed me that something had transpired of which I was as yet unaware, and I was adamant that he inform me of these new happenings. By his own admission, he requested my presence on his cases so that I might assist him in his investigations and provide a strong arm he could rely on in times of danger. But how could I hope to fulfill such expectations if he kept me perpetually in the dark.

"In good time, Watson," he said again. "Once we've boarded the train and settled ourselves, all will be revealed."

Holmes's penchant for dramatically heightening the tension of an investigation could at times be maddening.

"Are we ready to travel, Jessup?" Lord Silverpin asked.

"We are, indeed, my Lord," Jessup replied. He opened the door to the hall, and I saw that two coaches were waiting.

Jessup then called out these instructions; "Staunton will drive Lord Silverpin and Lady Vivienne, Mr. Holmes, and Dr. Watson in the first coach. Gladney, you will follow with myself, Alexander, and the women."

At the mention of the elusive coachman, whom I assumed had fled to avoid Holmes's interrogation; I plucked at Holmes's sleeve. "Staunton is here," I whispered urgently. "Will you not confront him now, before he can do any more harm?"

Holmes gave a curt shake of his head. "Not now," he said under his breath. "Do not excite yourself. All is in hand."

After Staunton and Gladney had hurried the baggage to the coaches, Lord Silverpin lifted an object covered with a lap rug from a table near the door and carried it out of the house. Holmes followed close upon his heels and as they crossed the gravel to the coach Holmes stumbled, catching hold of the object in Lord Silverpin's hands to steady himself. In doing so, the drape was dislodged, and I saw beneath it an elaborately decorated Egyptian box. Holmes apologized to Lord Silverpin for his clumsiness, quickly replaced the drape, and we boarded our assigned conveyances.

As we drove along, Lord Silverpin narrated the history of their house and lands, telling us fascinating stories of the surrounding countryside. One such story described how an entire village had been relocated in order for Highmount House to be constructed. So entertaining were the young Lord's narratives that the trip seemed to take no time at all, and the next thing I knew we had arrived at Whitchurch station. Holmes, on the other hand, had been distracted the entire journey. I had observed him periodically opening a window, poking his head out, and peering about in all directions. I thought of the watchers, patted the service revolver nestled in my pocket, and wondered if we were being followed.

The Silverpins' train had been brought to the platform and was being prepared. The train consisted of an engine, a coal car, a salon car, a baggage car, and cars for the coaches and horses. I had never before traveled on a private train and did not know what to expect. I needn't have worried. Every necessity had been anticipated. The trip would not be a long one since we would be making no other stops along the way.

Staunton attempted to relieve Lord Silverpin of the Egyptian box, but he refused and carried it into the salon car. Lady Vivienne and I climbed in after him. The domestic staff followed, while Staunton and Gladney went to work loading the baggage, coaches, and horses. Holmes had slipped away and was engaged in conversation with the station master. I tried to get Holmes's attention but could not distract him. I called for the porter and impressed upon the man that under no circumstances should the train be allowed to leave if Mr. Holmes were not on board. It wasn't long before the whistle blew indicating the engineer was ready to depart. I looked anxiously out the window and saw Holmes vigorously shaking the station master's hand before sprinting across the platform just as the whistle sounded again.

Holmes joined me at a table in the salon car. The tables were covered with white linen cloths. The table settings were the finest bone china, sterling plate, and each had a small vase of fresh flowers. I could not imagine where they had gotten these exotic blooms in the middle of winter.

"Orchids from the conservatory," Holmes remarked as if reading my thoughts, which he often seemed able to do.

"Ah," I said, "of course."

"Gentlemen," Lord Silverpin addressed us as he and Lady Vivienne seated themselves at our table. "I trust you slept well, and that you, Mr. Holmes, have recovered from your assault."

"I am in fine fettle, your Lordship," Holmes replied. "I thank you for your concern."

"I am well enough," said I. In truth, I had slept fitfully, thoughts of the watchers intruding upon my peace.

"I am glad to hear it," said Lady Vivienne.

While we exchanged pleasantries with the Silverpins, Jessup and the maid of all work served us coffee and pastries before removing themselves to the opposite end of the car to join the other servants for their own breakfast. Staunton and Gladney were with the horses and because there was no communication between the cars, would have to do without breakfast unless they had packed a basket.

Lady Vivienne took a sip from her cup and looked keenly at Holmes. "Mr. Holmes, have you anything to report?"

Holmes held a finger to his lips and glanced furtively at the servants' table.

"While you were boarding," said he in a low voice, "I spoke with the porter and the station master. Early in the morning on the day your father disappeared, the porter saw a man he believed to be the Earl with Staunton. Now, I remind you of what Jim Gladney said. Both men were completely muffled against the cold, their faces barely visible. The porter spoke only to Staunton. He had only Staunton's declaration that the man accompanying him was the Earl. The station master did not speak with Staunton or the other man. He got his information from the porter. Neither had any reason to question what Staunton told them, hence, their statements to the police. We know now with almost complete certainty that the person with Staunton was not the Earl. They arrived at such an early hour so the person masquerading as the Earl could board without encountering the regular train crew who would surely recognize him."

I had to concede Holmes's analysis of the situation was, as always, eminently plausible.

"And, I have just now received a reply in response to my telegram to Scotland Yard," said Holmes. "Inspector Crowe and his men will be at the platform when we arrive. They will take Staunton into custody."

I was relieved that Holmes had finally enlightened us to his plans. Obviously, he wanted to take Staunton by surprise in London rather than trusting his confinement and questioning to the local constabulary. All that remained a mystery now was the contents of the Egyptian box. I had my suspicions, but it would have been inappropriate of me to query Lord Silverpin.

Holmes bid us go about the rest of the trip as if we knew nothing of what awaited Staunton once we reached London. Lord Silverpin and Lady Vivienne amused themselves with a game of chess. Jessup and his staff were engaged in a game of cards, all the while keeping a watchful eye on their employers should any need arise. I spent my time with my feet up, reading, while Holmes sat nearby at one of the windows quietly smoking his pipe and gazing out at the countryside as we rolled by.

Two hours later, we pulled into the London station. When the coaches and horses had been taken off the cars and we had all disembarked, Staunton came across the platform towards us. I saw Holmes glance to his left, and it was then that four men, three uniformed officers and one in plain clothes, moved quickly to surround Staunton and take hold of him. Staunton cried out and struggled. The detective who identified himself as Inspector Aloysius Crowe informed the coachman that he was being taken into custody on suspicion of the kidnapping and possible murder of the Right Honorable Robert Henry, the Fifth Earl of Convarran. Staunton stared a moment as if he could not comprehend what had been said to him. Then all the color drained from his face. He struggled against his captors and managed to turn to Lord Silverpin.

"My Lord," he said, "you cannot believe I would do anything against your family. I am innocent of the crime of which these men have accused me."

"I do not want to believe it," Lord Silverpin said. "But there are witnesses against you and we must, for our father's sake, get to the bottom of this terrible affair."

"Witnesses against me," Staunton cried. His wild eyes fell on Holmes. "Is it you who have poisoned my master's mind against me?" The coachman made to lunge at Holmes. But the three constables quickly got him under control and took him away.

Lord Silverpin and Lady Vivienne stood upon the platform looking completely bereft. The servants, their faces bearing signs of shock, gathered around their employers as if to protect them.

"Lord Silverpin," said Holmes, "you and Lady Vivienne must go directly to Mayfair."

"Of course," replied Lord Silverpin.

"The danger is grave," said Holmes. "Do not leave or receive anyone; do not accept any communication until Watson and I join you. My mind will rest more easily if you will do as I say."

It was Lavinia Stoddard, Lady Vivienne's personal maid, who broke the spell.

"Come now, your Ladyship," she said. "We mustn't stand about like common folk; let us go on to your townhouse." With that, she took her mistress by the arm and led her to the coach where Alexander, Lord Silverpin's valet, was in animated, urgent communication with Jim Gladney regarding who would drive the second coach.

"If we may be of assistance," said Holmes. "I have coach driving experience. Watson and I shall be happy to drive the second coach."

Relief brightened both men's faces.

"Holmes ..." I interjected.

"Come along, Watson," said he as he swung up onto the box. I scrambled up next to him as he called out to the groom, "Lead the way, young Jim, and we shall follow."

"Right you are, Mr. Holmes," Gladney called back. He leaped up onto his coach, snapped his whip above the horses' backs and cried, "Go along, boys!" And so, we set off at a trot for Mayfair.

Holmes had not exaggerated his ability. He drove like a professional cabbie negotiating snarls in the traffic and deftly avoiding pedestrians while hardly slowing our pace. After arriving at the Silverpins' Mayfair residence, its exquisite façade outstanding even on this street of elegant homes, we relinquished the coach to the care of Jim Gladney, assuring the Silverpins that we would return in all haste once Holmes had attended to the business immediately at hand, namely perusing the responses to his numerous communications and arranging for a visit to Scotland Yard and Inspector Crowe. Public conveyances in Mayfair were by no means hard to come by, and in minutes of taking our leave, we were ensconced in a hackney cab on our way to Baker Street.

Chapter Thirteen

At one o'clock, we presented ourselves at Scotland Yard determined to extract from Staunton that information which would lead us to Robert Henry the Fifth Earl of Convarran. Inspector Aloysius Crowe was awaiting us, and I reckoned we would find out soon enough if he would help or hinder our investigation.

"Mr. Holmes and Dr. Watson, if I'm not mistaken," he greeted us, proffering his hand. "Your reputation precedes you."

"At your service," Holmes replied, grasping Crowe's hand and shaking it vigorously.

I, in turn, shook his hand, but I still wasn't sure I liked the look of him. Call it intuition if you will. There was something off about the man. He was of medium height, clean-shaven, with dark hair and remarkably handsome features. I noted that he dressed quite a bit more fashionably than the other detectives. Savile Row, if I didn't miss my guess. He had piercing blue eyes and a rather disconcerting way of staring directly at whomever he was speaking with, obviously sizing up his subject. Holmes appeared not to notice, but the intensity of the inspector's scrutiny nonplussed me. Perhaps as a policeman he could get away with it, but in polite society, it would be considered impossibly rude.

"I understand Inspector Lestrade has been reassigned," said Holmes.

"That's correct," said Inspector Crowe. "His previous cases have been parceled out and his sole focus now is to look into these latest Whitechapel murders. He's got his hands full to be sure. Inspector Lestrade spoke highly of you and advised me to cooperate with you."

"Did he now?" said Holmes. "We appreciate his confidence, I'm sure." A smile flickered upon his lips.

The Inspector brought two chairs from unoccupied desks and bade us sit.

"Have you questioned Staunton?"

"I have, Mr. Holmes."

"Does he still protest his innocence?"

"He does not. He has confessed."

At this statement, Holmes leaned forward. "Has he?"

"What?" I cried. "Just yesterday he swore to his innocence, and all but accused Holmes of framing him."

"Am I correct in surmising that you have not yet conveyed this information to your superiors?" asked Holmes.

Crowe glanced at the surrounding desks. There were no other inspectors nearby and those who were in the room were engaged in conversation.

"You are correct, Mr. Holmes."

"Why ever not?" I exclaimed.

Holmes answered: "Because, Watson, the inspector does not believe Staunton's confession is valid."

"It's just as you say, Mr. Holmes. If informed my superiors will readily accept his confession and act upon it with all haste."

"To what did Staunton confess?" asked Holmes.

"He confessed to the abduction and murder of the Right Honorable Robert Henry, Fifth Earl of Convarran."

I could not help but gasp at the revelation.

"What reason have you to believe he may be innocent of involvement in the Earl's disappearance and possibly his death?" asked Holmes.

"Not innocent of involvement," Crowe replied, "but perhaps innocent of responsibility."

"You believe Staunton was forced to participate in the Earl's abduction and murder through some threat to himself or others?" I asked.

"Not exactly, Doctor," continued Inspector Crowe. He drew a long breath then released it slowly. "When Staunton tells his story, it's always the same. He says the words, but he speaks without any feeling, and at times he even seems confused by what he's said. If you ask him specifically about the Earl, a queer look comes into his eyes. If you press him upon a point, he becomes agitated, even aggressive. He won't say where the killing took place, how he managed it, or what he did with the body. Only that he did it. Change the subject and his demeanor becomes calm."

Holmes looked at Crowe intently. "That the Earl is dead is speculation," said he. "There is no evidence thus far to substantiate that. Do you have a theory, Inspector?"

"Of a sort. Staunton's behavior puts me in mind of another case I investigated some years ago that involved a magician and mesmerism, or as it's called now, hypnotic suggestion. Now bear in mind, that situation was not to the degree that we have here, but the symptoms as I understand them are similar."

"Mesmerism," I muttered. "Stuff and nonsense. A parlor trick pulled off by spiritualists, conjurers, and card-readers. You can see it all in any music hall. Men and women strutting about crowing like roosters, barking like dogs, all at the charlatan's so-called command. Ringers one and all. You're not suggesting …"

"Hypnotic suggestion," said Holmes, cutting me off, "is a new study in the West. A few physicians, such as yourself, have begun to study its usefulness as an anesthetic for medical procedures. Do you not recall the article I pointed out to you in *The Times* recently concerning that Parisian woman, Gabrielle Bompard? The popular presses call her the Little Demon. She is charged with the murder of a prominent financier, Toussaint-Agustin Gouffé. Her defense is that she acted under the control of a sadistic hypnotist. The investigation has launched an international manhunt for this hypnotist, Michel Eyraud. The trial will no doubt be filled with drama. We will be witness to two rival schools of thought: Jules Liégeois, the world's leading expert on hypnosis and crime for the defense, versus Jean Martin Charcot for the prosecution. Liégeois asserts that Mlle. Bompard was made a pawn, controlled against her will, to commit murder. Charcot declares just as emphatically that committing murder under hypnosis is impossible."

"A ruse to avoid the noose," said I.

"And if it isn't?" Holmes countered.

"Good lord," I said. "Are you suggesting this could be done to anyone?"

"No, Doctor," Crowe replied. "Not everyone is suggestible, and those who are vary in intensity of effect based on their degree of susceptibility and the skill of the practitioner. Some persons, it seems, are not susceptible at all, and therefore cannot be hypnotized."

"So," said Holmes. "Returning to our case. If you are correct, then the hypnotist would almost certainly have had to have prior knowledge of Staunton's susceptibility, or the risk would have been too great."

"I believe that to be true, Mr. Holmes."

"Are you saying that you believe Staunton acted under hypnotic suggestion and abducted the Earl and murdered him?" I asked.

"I am no expert, Doctor. However, I intend to seek professional confirmation of Staunton's condition and the veracity of my theory from an alienist with experience in these matters."

"Excellent," said Holmes. "I believe I can assist you with that. I have a connection with Dr. T. B. Hyslop at Bethlehem Royal Hospital. He is experimenting with hypnotism as a means to treat disorders of the mind."

"I'd be much obliged, Mr. Holmes," Crowe said. "Now, before I take you to speak with Staunton, shall we review the report from the British Museum regarding the scarabs?"

"I am all ears, Inspector," said Holmes.

"In short, as I mentioned in my telegram, the examiners cannot identify the substance of which the bodies of the scarabs are composed. The substance is unknown and may possibly not be of this Earth."

"Meteoric rock is certainly a possibility," said Holmes. "But let us not forget that new mineral discoveries are made every day. This material may simply be something earthbound but not yet catalogued."

"An excellent point, Mr. Holmes," said Crowe with a slight smile.

"The examiners found that, in darkness, the scarabs — or rather the substance from which the scarabs were created — exhibits a green luminescence."

"Such luminescence can occur naturally," Holmes replied.

"As for your observation about the hieroglyphs engraved upon the scarabs — let me read from the examiner's report: 'This is an effect produced by facets within the substance itself and a skilled artisan might make use of such knowledge to produce a dramatic effect such as you experienced.' The examiners also found that 'the substance absorbs heat from the body and other heat sources, such as sunlight or fire, and by some internal means amplifies it, giving the impression that the scarab itself is generating heat.'"

This concluded Inspector Crowe's reading of the report and he returned the document to his desk.

"What of the feelings of anxiety I experienced?" I asked. "You did include that in your report, didn't you Holmes?

The feeling began as anxiety, quickly progressed to dread, and at the last, was full-on panic!"

"I did convey that to the examiners," said Holmes.

"There is nothing about that in the report," said the inspector. "The examiners' final remark is: 'As for the substance's, shall we say, other properties, our findings are inconclusive.'"

"Inconclusive! It was not my imagination; I can assure you!" I remarked rather huffily.

"What was your experience of the scarabs, Inspector, if I might inquire?" asked Holmes.

"I have not seen them, Mr. Holmes. They were packed up and sent off to the British Museum before I arrived. However, I have requested that they be returned to police custody forthwith, and I will examine them then."

"I shall be interested in hearing your observations," said Holmes.

Inspector Crowe rose from his desk. "Very good, gentlemen. If you're ready, I'll take you down to the cells."

"A moment, Inspector," said Holmes. "I feel obliged to inform you of a recent development. The Silverpins have received a communication that appears to be from the Earl."

"What?" cried Inspector Crowe. "When?"

"Yesterday," said Holmes, removing the missive from his pocket and handing it to the Inspector. "The Silverpins have attested to the handwriting being that of their father, and a comparison from extensive samples appears to bear out that conclusion."

The inspector perused the letter closely before returning it to Holmes. "How do you and your clients intend to respond?" he asked.

"We intend to use the situation to our advantage, and I suggest that the police join forces with us in this endeavor as it presents a good probability of apprehending the miscreants. I propose all parties meet; we can engage in a council of war and coordinate our efforts. I will interview Matheson when he returns and seek his assistance as it will be near impossible to carry off such an operation without it."

Inspector Crowe nodded, his eyes narrowed, and he fixed Holmes with an intense gaze. "I'll trust you to make the arrangements, Mr. Holmes, and you *will* keep me informed of all developments. I can't have civilians working at cross purposes with the police."

On this, they shook hands. "Of course," said Holmes. His steely grey eyes matched the intensity of the inspector's scrutiny.

"And now," said Inspector Crowe turning his attention away from Holmes, "shall we see about Staunton?"

We followed the inspector to a dreary passage lined with iron doors. The inspector slid open a small panel in the door to Staunton's cell through which one could communicate with the prisoner.

"I'll not go in with you," he said in a low voice. "I'd like to listen without his being aware of my presence."

He peered through the opening before instructing the guard to station himself outside until we were done. He then stepped aside and motioned to the guard to unlock the cell. We peered into the dim cavity where Staunton, still in his coachman's livery, lay upon his back on a stone slab. We were obliged to stand as there was nowhere to sit. Staunton remained prone and listless, refusing to acknowledge our presence.

"I am Sherlock Holmes and this is Dr. Watson. You may recall meeting us at Highmount House. We are employed by Lord Silverpin and Lady Vivienne to find their father."

This statement was met with silence.

"Inspector Crowe tells me that you have confessed to abducting and killing your master. He does not believe you are guilty, and he has opened my mind to that possibility."

"Then you are both fools," Staunton mumbled before turning his back to us.

I had been observing Staunton for the signs Inspector Crowe had mentioned. I was thwarted in my efforts as the man refused to look us in the eyes; he would not even raise his head. Holmes, not to be deterred, pressed on.

"What possible reason could you have for abducting and destroying your master?"

Staunton twitched.

"The Highmount police believe you were paid to abduct him," Holmes continued.

Again, Staunton did not reply.

"And yet," Holmes persisted. "No money was discovered on your person, nor found in your room, nor were there any items discovered that you might have purchased with such a payment. You've not been spending on drink as I've inquired at the Blue Boar in Highmount. You have no relations that require your support."

Staunton did not move. My temper getting the better of me, I stepped forward and shouted.

"Sit up, man. Answer Mr. Holmes when you're spoken to, or I'll drag you up myself! He is trying to save you from the noose."

Staunton rolled over, pushed himself up, and regarded us with a sullen face. He grimaced and shook his head as if to clear it.

"The Earl was a hard master. He got what he deserved."

"Pshaw," said Holmes. "It was no trouble for me to ascertain through the confidential admissions of those in service that there is no better place to serve than Highmount House. The merest whisper of a vacancy would result in a deluge of applications from men and women — many employed at other great houses — who would give their eye teeth to secure such a position."

Staunton started to rock rhythmically back and forth. Here at last was a sign of agitation.

"I ask you again," said Holmes in a stern, clipped voice, "what induced you to harm the Earl and betray Lord Silverpin?"

At the word betray, Staunton cried out, leapt from his slab, and flung himself at Holmes, catching him by the lapels.

Expecting to see fury in the man's eyes, I was for a moment taken aback for there was no fury — only that dull inward-turning stare the inspector had described. Nevertheless, the grip he had upon my friend was a deadly one and I rushed to Holmes's aid. I shouted for the guard who, upon hearing Staunton's cry, had rammed the key in the lock and now burst through the door with his truncheon raised. In the intervening moments, I had got my arm round Staunton's neck in a choke hold which I applied forcefully. As the guard maneuvered to strike a blow, Staunton went limp. I released my hold on him, and he dropped to his knees and keeled over.

Holmes grasped Staunton by his coat and hauled him to his feet, whereupon he slapped the man's face several times with vigor. Staunton seemed not to feel it.

"You did not kill the Earl. Speak the truth, man!"

Staunton gripped his head in his hands and moaned as if afflicted with great pain. "No … I … I did …"

"Well, well. Never mind," said Holmes releasing him.

Staunton staggered back and sat down hard upon the ledge.

"Would you like a cup of tea?" asked Holmes.

I can barely credit the transformation that occurred when Holmes uttered that phrase. Staunton became instantly calm, his features placid, the tension left his limbs, and he gazed at Holmes with the look of an adoring dog.

"Yes," he murmured. "Tea would be most welcome."

Inspector Crowe came into the cell and exchanged a knowing look with Holmes.

"I shall see to your tea, Staunton," Crowe said.

"Thank you, sir," Staunton replied. He once again turned his back to us and curled up upon the stone slab where we had originally found him.

As we exited the cell and made our way back to the inspectors' area, Holmes asked, "How long have we?"

"A day, maybe two. I dare not withhold his confession any longer."

Holmes nodded as his lips settled into a grim line. "It is not enough time."

A shadow passed over Holmes's face and he turned abruptly to Inspector Crowe. "Has anyone been here to see him?"

"Not that I am aware of, Mr. Holmes," Inspector Crowe replied. He cast an inquiring look at the guard accompanying us.

The man shook his head and replied: "No, sir, not on my watch, sir."

"Check with the other guards and report back," Crowe snapped. "No one sees him without my permission. Understood?"

The guard gave a curt nod. "Understood, sir."

As we left Scotland Yard and passed through the arch and into Great Scotland Yard Street in search of our cabbie, I ventured a question even though my friend's expression was all thunder and lightning.

"You believe, then, that Staunton is innocent?"

Holmes jabbed his stick in the air. "You saw the man, Watson. Give me a motive, any motive that is credible, and I shall reconsider."

Chapter Fourteen

On the second day after our visit to Scotland Yard, I arose to find Holmes by the fire perusing his crime indexes, a cloud of stinking tobacco smoke swirling above his head. This was a sure indication he'd been there all night. He leapt suddenly from his chair and rushed to his desk whereupon he began to scribble some dispatch at a furious pace. He then made for the door and shouted for Billy, our pageboy. In the previous twenty-four hours, Billy had traversed the stair a dozen times a day delivering and dispatching telegrams, letters, and parcels.

After our meeting with Inspector Crowe and the explosive interview with Staunton, Holmes became a dynamo of activity, so much so that I feared for his health. I had no doubt he was hot on a scent for he came and went at all hours and barely slept or ate. However, any attempt to advise my friend against such strenuous, uninterrupted activity, he waved off with shouts of "Time, Watson! Time is our enemy!"

No sooner had Billy departed with Holmes's latest communication than there came a clanging of the bell followed by a riotous clamor upon the stairs accompanied by Mrs. Hudson's strident protestations. Before they had even tumbled through our door, I knew them to be the Baker Street Irregulars, that gang of ragged street urchins that Holmes employed when he had need of wide-ranging, invisible surveillance.

I knew that Holmes had engaged the services of the Irregulars to keep watch on the Silverpins' Mayfair residence.

Where else they might be stationed, I couldn't say, but there were at least three teams working in shifts round the clock with their commander, Wiggins, delivering daily reports. I felt sorry for these youngsters, rough and unruly as they might be, as few were dressed sufficiently against the biting cold. A few were barefoot, their feet wrapped in rags. When Holmes employed them, he paid them handsomely for their efforts and that at least kept some meat on their bones.

A rag-tag group of six boys swarmed into our rooms. Stamping their feet and rubbing their hands together, they gathered around Holmes who greeted them amiably and urged them closer to the fire where they commenced warming their fronts and their backsides. I knew Wiggins, but the other five I did not recognize. Their hair, sticking out from beneath cloth caps and bowlers too large for their heads, was unkempt and badly cut. All five were sniffling and wiping runny noses on their sleeves. They ranged in age from quite young to early teens and all were filthy with dirt. All but Wiggins regarded us with a wary eye.

One of the youngest and smallest was stained with soot, a dreadful clue to his recent employment. The practice of using children as chimney sweeps had been outlawed in 1875 after the death of twelve-year-old George Brewster in the chimneys of Fulbourn Hospital. Even so, there were still unscrupulous men in the foulest parts of the city who continued the abuse at the risk of their own freedom. I shuddered at the thought of the boys forced to climb into those narrow, stifling shafts, every breath filling their lungs with poisonous black dust.

"Watson," Holmes said, "go down and apologize to Mrs. Hudson for the disturbance and beseech her for a tea tray and make sure there are plenty of biscuits. Bring it up yourself. No sense in causing the poor woman any further agitation. There's a good fellow."

When I returned, laboring under the weight of a tray piled high with tea, crockery, milk, and cakes, Holmes had the children sitting cross-legged round the fire. There was an audible intake of breath when they realized the repast I was bearing was intended for them. They jumped to their feet with arms outstretched before I had time to set down the tray.

"'ere now!" shouted Wiggins. "'old on! You lot sit down and wait your turns."

They hesitated, shuffled their feet, a few grumbled, but at a fierce look from Wiggins, the boys settled back into their places by the fire.

"Excellent!" exclaimed Holmes. "Come along, Watson; help me distribute this bounty to our guests."

For a good ten minutes, not a word was uttered, only the sounds of tea being slurped from cups and the smacking of lips as cakes were devoured. The older boys amused themselves by extending their pinky fingers, pointing their noses at the ceiling, and sipping their tea through puckered lips as they aped how they imagined "the toffs" looked taking their tea. When the last drops had been drained from the pots and hardly a crumb remained, Wiggins addressed Holmes.

"Beggin' your pardon, Mr. 'olmes, I know you don't like 'avin' the rank and file underfoot, but I've 'ad to take on extra crew to keep an eye on all these folk. These 'ere are the new ones: Raven, 'awk, Dodger, Littlejohn, and Mouse. They seen your picture in the papers, Mr. 'olmes, and wanted to reckon for themselves if you were the real thing."

"And are you satisfied?" Holmes asked them.

There was a universal nodding of heads and murmurs of assent.

"Well then," said Holmes. "I, too, am satisfied. If Wiggins vouches for you, his word is good enough for me." He reached into his coat pocket and brought out a handful of coins and handed a shilling to each boy.

"Now, then," said he, "that is an advance. Wiggins will distribute your pay in future. Once you have your orders, you can begin your tasks. Wiggins will stay awhile and report last night's progress."

"Just so you know, Mr. 'olmes, the forecast is callin' for perishin' cold tonight and another snowstorm possible. If that's what we get, I can't ask the lads to endure it, no matter the pay."

Five dirty, expectant, faces looked up at my friend. Holmes frowned, and then nodded. "Let us pray then that the fairer weather holds."

Coins disappeared into pockets as Wiggins rousted his crew and herded them to the door. "I'll set them off, Mr. 'olmes, and be right back."

While Holmes waited for Wiggins to return, I gathered up the tea things and carried them down to Mrs. Hudson's kitchen. I met Wiggins on my way back and we came up the stairs together.

"Look here, Wiggins," I said pulling some notes from my pocketbook and pressing them into his hands. "Those boys without shoes, they're vulnerable to frostbite. Do you think you could get them some shoes and some stockings, as well?"

Wiggins stared at the notes in his hands. For a moment, some strong emotion played across his features. "I will," said he. "Thank you, Doctor."

When we came back into our sitting room, Holmes was in his chair by the fire.

"Come, sit, Wiggins. What have you to tell me?"

"Well," said Wiggins, curling into the basket chair. "First off, that gent, Matheson, 'e come 'ome last night."

"Excellent," Holmes said. "Watson, pass me a sheet of paper, an envelope, and my pen. Thank you."

I did as he requested, and he placed the paper upon the back of one of his indexes and wrote out a note which he then folded and placed in the envelope. He addressed it to: Mr. Cedric Matheson, 61 North Worple Way, Mortlake, London SW. He sealed the envelope, and I passed him a stamp.

"Wiggins," he said, handing him the letter. "Would you be so good as to post this in the nearest box immediately upon leaving?"

Wiggins took the letter and slipped it into a pocket of his threadbare coat. "Consider it done, Mr. 'olmes."

"Now," said Holmes, "let us move on. What activity have you observed at the Mayfair house?"

"There are three dark men, foreigners of some sort, lurking about. Only one at a time though. Keep themselves well 'idden, they do."

"Where do they watch?"

"At the trades door, Mr. 'olmes."

"Are they watching for a particular person?"

"''ard to say what they're after. They've made no other move. At least not yet."

"And what of Professor Emm's residence?"

"Some rough lookin' folk comin' and going'. "

"Are they servants?"

"If that gang is servants, then I'm a monkey's uncle. Cut purses, footpads, and worse is more like. They come and go at all 'ours and they're not about any servants' work."

"And you've not seen the Professor?"

"Not a bit of 'im, sir."

"And Dr. Scarabus?"

"Followed 'im to some low establishments, we did. Last night, a private carriage picked 'im up from 'is house. No markings. Carried 'im off to the Running Footman. 'e waits for a man to come. They talk and pass each other parcels, secret like, and then the man leaves. Scarabus waits a spell, and then 'e takes 'is leave. The driver takes off like 'e 'as the devil after 'im. Topper nearly broke 'is 'ead tryin' to jump on the back. We lost 'im, and 'e ain't come 'ome yet."

"What does this man look like?" Holmes asked.

Wiggins stretched himself and yawned. No doubt the lad was exhausted from his labors on Holmes's behalf.

"I can't rightly say, Mr. 'olmes. 'e was bundled up to his ears. Didn't even take 'is 'at off. About as tall as you. Smooth 'ands. Not seen any 'ard work, that 'un. Mean eyes and always lookin' over 'is shoulder.

"Indeed," said Holmes. "I'll accompany you on your surveillance of Dr. Scarabus this evening."

Wiggins stood. "Very good, Mr. 'olmes. Dr. Scarabus, 'e don't move durin' the day. I'll come by for you tonight, around nine, if the weather 'olds." He started toward the door, then paused a moment and turned. "I reckon you know it already. There's a man watching this 'ouse. Spied 'im as we came in."

My blood ran cold as I recalled the watchers at Highmount House and the attack upon Holmes. "What!" I cried. "Where is the wretch? I'll put him to rout!"

"Calm yourself, Watson. We will let him remain. Let him think we are unaware of his presence. One of Wiggins' lieutenants can keep an eye on him."

"'e's one ov' 'em so-called servants of Professor Emm," Wiggins said. "Been 'angin' about since you got back."

"Well, well," Holmes murmured. "Go out the back way, Wiggins. Keep out of sight until you're clear of Baker Street."

Chapter Fifteen

We arrived at the home of Cedric Matheson, the great adventurer, a few minutes after noon. The butler showed us into the study where we found the gentleman himself. Matheson was a large man by anyone's standards. And by large, I do not mean corpulent. The man was a bruiser, all muscle and energy. His rugged features were enhanced by a deep tan that could only have come from an extended time in the tropics. His dark, wavy hair was thick, touched with grey at the temples.

"It's hardly afternoon. The clock has only just struck twelve," he exclaimed. "I expected you later in the day. I've made arrangements with Nicky to collect those crates, and then I'm off to the Egyptian Hall. I am organizing everything today. So, as I'm sure you can see, I've little time to spare."

It took me a moment to realize that Matheson was referring to Lord Silverpin, whose Christian name is Nicholas Alexander Henry.

"Your time will not be wasted," said Holmes acerbically. "I take it you have had a communication from the Earl of Convarran?"

"I have," said Matheson. "He's explained his absence; so, gentlemen, it appears he's no longer missing. And in that case, perhaps you will let me get on with my business."

"We believe that communication to be a forgery or coerced, and you, like the Silverpins, may be in the gravest danger."

Holmes then proceeded to advise Matheson of our investigation and impressed upon him that his insight was vital to a successful conclusion to our case. Matheson frowned at that but agreed to delay his departure.

"I'll answer your questions, Mr. Holmes. I'll tell you as I told Inspector Crowe — I have nothing to hide."

"Good heavens," I said. "Has Inspector Crowe been here already?"

"At first light, blast him," said Matheson. "Though how he knew I returned last night, I cannot imagine unless he has had my house under surveillance."

"It is entirely likely," said Holmes with the hint of a smile.

The room in which we found ourselves might have been a museum. It was crammed with all manner of unusual weaponry, hunting trophies, and strange artifacts, few of which were familiar to me. I assumed these were memorabilia from his many forays into the wilds of exotic countries. His exploits had been widely chronicled by himself and others. His name was a household word.

He motioned for us to take seats by the fire while he fetched a decanter of whisky which he offered us, and we accepted. He poured out three glasses, and then poked at the fire until he turned over some embers whereupon he put on another log and waited for it to catch fire. He tugged at his high, stiff collar, loosening its grip upon his neck, and then proceeded to undo his tie and shrug off his coat. He saw me observing him and gave me a wry look, before draining his glass in one swallow.

"I am no longer used to this claptrap. It constrains me, as does all of this society. It won't be a moment too soon that I'm back in the field; there are no such contrivances there."

Holmes began his interview. "Perhaps, you could begin by telling us who or what you believe to be behind the disappearances of the Earl of Convarran, possibly Professor Emm, and the murder of Sir Roger Trumbull."

"You get right to the point, Mr. Holmes, I'll give you that," said Matheson settling himself into a chair with a frame and armrests constructed of elephant tusks. "But I must ask you why you think I can tell you anything as I have been out of the country and only recently heard of these events."

"You can tell us what happened in Dahshoor."

Matheson started to speak, but Holmes forestalled him. "You should know that I have read the Earl's private journal. He wrote that the expedition abandoned the dig at Dahshoor because there was nothing there worth excavating. He also stated that Emm was not in accord with this conclusion. In addition, he wrote that he had recently received intelligence about the location of an unmolested tomb in the Valley of the Kings and that he intended to mount an expedition there as soon as time and finances would allow."

"That much is true," said Matheson.

"Indeed," said Holmes. "But that was not the only reason for your hasty departure. You, the Earl, and Sir Roger had already decided to leave Dahshoor before the Earl learned about this other tomb. Why?"

Matheson bristled and leaned forward in his chair. "For the very reasons you've just mentioned, and I've confirmed!

Digs are abandoned all the time. There's nothing strange in that. It's no different than speculating on a gold mine. Some pan out and others don't. Only a fool keeps pecking away when every sign tells him to pack up and move on. If not for that reason, then what reason do you surmise, Mr. Holmes?"

"The Black Pharaoh, perhaps," said Holmes.

Those words brought about a profound alteration in Matheson's demeanor. He gripped the arms of his chair, then grabbed the whisky decanter and poured himself another glass.

"Pray tell us all you know," said Holmes.

After the jolt Holmes had given him, Matheson appeared to recover quickly. I was not surprised as his occupation fairly demanded quick thinking and reflexes. How else had he survived the ordeals he'd endured during his many dangerous exploits?

"Well, well," said he. "I'll tell you about my part in that ill-fated expedition, Mr. Holmes. I don't know how you've come to know about the Black Pharaoh—from Robert's journal, I suppose, though I'm surprised he wrote about it … any of it."

"You are referring to the plan to abandon Emm to his fate in Cairo sans resources," Holmes said. "It is imperative we hear the details firsthand from you, beginning to end."

"If it will help find Robert and bring his abductors to justice, I will spare the time. Robert is a good man and a plain dealer. I count him as a friend."

"Thank you," said Holmes. "Pray tell us how you came to select Dahshoor as a dig site?"

"A moment," said Matheson as he pulled a bell cord, a tiger's tail, that hung near his chair. Within moments of his doing so, a dark-skinned, turbaned Sikh appeared dressed in native attire. He bowed, and then asked, "What is your wish, Sahib?"

"Inform Lord Silverpin that I am delayed and will join him later this afternoon."

The Sikh bowed and withdrew.

"My batman," said Matheson. "Fellow's indispensable in a tiger hunt." He lit an Indian Trichinopoly cigar and continued. "Anyway, it was the Professor who convinced Robert to dig at Dahshoor. The man could spin a yarn, I'll give him that. I had my doubts and I said so, but in the end, it was Robert's money, so we went. I knew the place. Hadn't been there, but I knew others who had. They allowed Dahshoor had possibilities — not like the Valley, of course, but worthwhile and with a little less competition. The pyramids there were built at the beginning of the Middle Kingdom; less grand perhaps than the mortuary temples and tombs constructed by the pharaohs of the late Middle Kingdom, but impressive nonetheless."

"Was there any trouble during your journey from England?"

"None. No delays. No illness. No mishaps. We arrived as fit as fleas, set up camp, and went right to work."

"And later?"

"All went well the first week or so and then the trouble started, and I'll be damned if I can reckon what the cause of it was. I have my suspicions, but that's all it is: suspicion."

"That is when the attacks began?"

"Yes, but more than that, sir, much more than that. First, Trumbull and I discovered a cache of mummies in a shaft. It was a significant find and boded well for the future. It is one of those mummies, a priest called Hor, I brought back for the exhibition."

"The Egyptian laws are stricter now on the removal of human remains, are they not?" I asked.

"The local Khedives are willing to overlook a few bits and bobs for a little gold," said Matheson.

"Never mind that, Watson. Pray continue, Mr. Matheson."

"As I was saying, we discovered the mummies, but Emm took no interest in them. His only interest was in penetrating the base of the Black Pyramid. He would expend effort on nothing else. But for all his work, he discovered nothing — or so we thought at the time — and it soon became a bone of contention among us. Later, it became clear that he was after something else that he was keeping secret from us. My suspicion is that he could not accomplish such a feat on his own — no money and no pedigree — and like all dishonorable people, he couldn't trust anybody. So, he gulled Robert and Trumbull, who I'm sure he looked upon as easy marks. But he didn't count on me, Mr. Holmes, he didn't count on me. I'd dealt with his kind before."

"Have you any idea what Emm was after?"

"Every ancient civilization has its dark legends, its black magic, and its monsters, Mr. Holmes."

"I have some small knowledge of such things, but it is not a subject of particular interest to me."

"Well, it was of particular interest to Emm. He was obsessed with it. Whatever he was searching for, you can be sure, had to do with that."

"How do you know this? Did Emm speak to you about it?"

"Hardly; the man was a clam. But I had a good rifle through his belongings while he was off on one of his little wanders. I looked through some of his notes. Couldn't make heads or tails of those, but I found a packet of correspondence between himself and a Dr. "S" that I could understand. They talked about a hidden tomb beneath the Black Pyramid. They believed the pharaoh who occupied that tomb was not the pharaoh who built the pyramid. The builder was Amenemhat III. This other pharaoh, Nophru-ka, was said to be evil. It was he who deposed Amenemhat III and proceeded to rule the kingdom as a tyrant. However, few, if any know of him because at some time after his death, Nophru-ka's name was erased from history to ensure that his atrocities and vile practices would not be remembered."

"Someone remembered," said Holmes.

"Someone always does," replied Matheson.

"And there is always someone who will misuse the knowledge," I added.

"Indeed, Doctor," said Matheson. "And that someone was Emm."

"You refer to the Professor in the past tense," said Holmes.

"That's right, Mr. Holmes. It fell to me to dispose of him. Robert was too tender, and Trumbull too cowardly."

"You believe he is dead?"

"I know he is dead, Mr. Holmes. I shot him."

"What!" I cried.

"Come now, Doctor. I can see you are a military man. You know the punishment for betrayal, for treason."

"But yours was an archaeological expedition, not a military campaign."

"Have you ever been in the jungle, Doctor?'

"I have. The Indian jungle is a fearful place."

"Then you know. In the jungle, every man is responsible for the security of his brothers."

Matheson rose abruptly from his chair and in some agitation paced back and forth over the massive tiger skin rug that lay before the hearth.

"If a man acts only in his own interest, he jeopardizes every other man in the party as well as the success of the whole party. If allowed to operate unchecked, that man spells disaster for all."

"What of the attacks upon your expedition?" Holmes asked.

"I cannot think but that they had everything to do with Emm. Either instigated by him to distract us from his treachery or because someone had got wind of what he was up to."

"If Emm is not behind this business with the Earl, then who is?" I cried.

"It cannot be Emm," Matheson said with a satisfied look on his face. "The man was dead when I left him for the crocodiles. I will swear to it. You have heard my account, Mr. Holmes, and I hope it satisfies you. Now, if there is nothing else, I would like to be on my way. If I'm to get to the Valley this coming season, I need investors."

My expression must have betrayed my feelings, for Matheson chuckled and said, "Why should I spend my own money, Doctor, if I can spend someone else's?"

At first, I thought he was making a joke, but I saw no glimmer of amusement in his eyes.

"Not just yet," said Holmes. "Were you aware that the Earl brought the artifacts that Emm uncovered back to England? And do you believe there is anything to this legend?"

Matheson hesitated at this and appeared to be choosing his words carefully.

"I did not know Robert had kept the artifacts, though I can't say I'm surprised. Never have I met a more curious man, except perhaps Emm. If you don't know it already, then I shall tell you: Robert believed all that Egyptian religion nonsense, really believed it. He intended to be buried in the Egyptian style."

Here, Matheson paused for a time, lost in thought, until he said at last, "I've seen things. In my travels to the most distant, darkest nooks and crannies of this world, I have seen things I cannot explain. But that isn't to say those things cannot be examined and explained. I have not gotten where I am today by cringing at superstitions or being warned off by legends."

Matheson urged us to rise.

"There is one more thing," said Holmes. "I need your help. And I hope you will not shrink from my plan to recover the Earl and capture his abductors."

Matheson dropped back into his chair, placed his cigar on a brass tray, then reached again for the whisky decanter, filled his glass and ours, then turned to Holmes.

"What is it you want me to do?"

Chapter Sixteen

After depositing the Silverpins, Holmes, and myself at the Egyptian Hall in Piccadilly for the mummy unwrapping exhibition, Jim Gladney drove off in search of a quiet spot to park the Silverpins' coach until he needed to collect us later in the evening. He was bundled up to his ears and armed with a basket of hot food and drink, and a stack of magazines of the penny dreadful variety.

My nerves were on edge. I could not help but wonder whether Holmes's plan to apprehend the Earl's abductors would succeed. For the rescheduled exhibition, Holmes had Matheson and the Silverpins entice the public by mentioning that artifacts discovered in a secret burial chamber in the Black Pyramid that were improperly removed would be on display at the Egyptian Hall for the first night only before being turned over to the British Museum. It would be the public's only chance to see these unusual and macabre objects before they disappeared into the museum's vaults.

Holmes had made certain that the watchers at Highmount, if they'd been present, had seen Lord Silverpin transporting the Egyptian chest containing the stone and papyrus to our London-bound train. Matheson had agreed to describe the artifacts in detail and weave a compelling narrative around them during his presentation so there could be no mistaking what was on display in the private viewing room. There were guards inside and outside both rooms and only bona fide investors and guests would be allowed to view the artifacts.

However, contrary to what would be announced to the public, the artifacts were not at the Egyptian Hall. They had never left Highmount House and were secured there in the Temple of the Osirans, watched over by the formidable Madame Neferuptah. A woman, who, I had discovered, possessed considerable resolve and cleverness. Of course, we had no idea when an attempt would be made on the artifacts, or even if the villains would take the bait, but, according to Holmes, we were prepared for every possibility. I was not so sure.

The façade of the Egyptian Hall was a sight to behold. Its main entrance was flanked by tall lotus columns. Above the entrance, three temple-like faux archways displayed tablets engraved with hieroglyphics. The archways were topped with winged cobras, and on either side of the central arch were magnificent statues of the ancient Egyptian god Osiris and his sister-wife, the goddess Isis. On the pavement in front of the building were displayed sandwich boards that advertised upcoming shows including a well-known female spiritualist, Ariadne Thee; Maskelyne & Cooke, magicians of some renown; and an interesting oddity, a freak show. For myself, while I had passed the Egyptian Hall many times, despite its reputation and the popularity of its attractions, I had yet to attend an event within its precincts.

Once inside, we were directed to a lecture room in which the mummy unwrapping was to take place. Seats for at least a hundred people had been assembled before a semi-circular stage. Most of the seats were filled, but we had no trouble finding ours as the front row was reserved for the Silverpins, their guests, and members of the press. At the back of the room, long, narrow tables held a variety of refreshments: champagne, punch, and all manner of sweets and savories. Attendants stood ready to fill glasses and plates. Clouds of fragrant smoke from cigarettes, cigars, and pipes swirled in tendrils through the audience — smoke so thick at times it seemed our London fogs had come inside.

The stage was set with a painted replica of a wall from within an Egyptian temple. There were also paintings of the Dahshoor pyramid complex and the Black Pyramid. We didn't have long to wait before Matheson appeared on stage to enthusiastic applause. He had costumed himself to resemble an ancient Egyptian priest replete with white linen robes and a leopard skin draped over one shoulder. He wore a thick, braided wig, and his eyes were smudged with kohl. If he was nervous, he did not show it — just the opposite, in fact. He regaled the audience with tales in which he described obstacles and terrors that he and his fellow adventurers encountered at nearly every turn in their efforts to find a way into the burial chamber of the Black Pyramid. The press men and a press woman left their seats and gathered in a knot at the foot of the stage, their notebooks open, and their pencils poised, eager for the first opportunity to bombard Matheson with questions. Matheson, amid their protests, sent them back to their seats. "Gentlemen and lady of the press, please return to your seats. I assure you, I will answer all your questions after the show." The reporters reluctantly returned to their seats and a few moments later, Matheson held up his hands. "And now ladies and gentlemen, the moment you've all been waiting for."

There was a flurry of excited exclamations among the attendees. Matheson signaled to an assistant off-stage. Two men appeared bearing the mummy covered with a purple velvet cloth with golden fringe. Clouds of incense from the stage added to a miasma already thick with tobacco smoke, the tang of sweat, and the cloying scent of perfume. Matheson had barely begun his presentation and already I longed to break free from the oppressive closeness of the room and into the open air. Attendants turned down the gas in the wall sconces. Only candles illuminated the stage. Matheson stepped up to the mummy and with a flourish swept away the velvet drape.

A sudden disturbance at the back of the lecture room caused the audience to turn as one to witness a man who had the bizarre appearance of an elderly scarecrow, and a small band of confederates rush down the central aisle. They made a dash for the stage where they set up a loud appeal, imploring Matheson to abandon his desecration of the dead and allow them to rest in peace.

"It is Mr. Walraven and his supporters from the EEF," Lady Vivienne whispered in my ear amid shouts of outrage from the audience.

Holmes stood abruptly, nearly overturning his chair. "Confound the man," he cried. "He has ruined everything!"

As men from the audience surrounded Walraven and his followers, out-shouting them and drowning out their protests, I observed an attendant slip from the room. As the audience became increasingly restive, I feared for the safety of the interlopers. Besieged on all sides, they had given up their protest and were cowering before their challengers, unable to escape. Suddenly, the doors to the lecture room flew open and a team of powerfully built men in dark city suits and bowler hats entered and shoved their way to the protesters. They took hold of them — rather roughly — I thought, and proceeded to remove them from the room, followed by a gaggle of pressman shouting questions at their backs. I wondered what Holmes had meant by his outburst. I intended to ask him, but when I looked around for him, I found he had gone.

Matheson called for order and urged those still milling about to return to their seats. When order had mostly been restored, he begged the crowd's pardon for the disturbance. After a few moments, Matheson raised his arms. A hush fell over the crowd.

Matheson first explained the mummy-making process to the audience. He then further titillated us by describing the amulets, charms, and other precious items that might be revealed as the layers of bandages were removed. He told us the name of the priest, Hor, whose mummy this was and what little was known of his life. He explained that Hor had been found with a cache of other mummies and that they may have been hidden to avoid desecration.

I glanced at the Silverpins who sat stony-faced, staring with disapprobation at the stage.

"Indeed," said Lady Vivienne under her breath. "Hidden to avoid the very desecration you are about to perform."

I wondered again what had become of Holmes.

The crowd, eager for the unwrapping to begin, and having consumed a good deal of spirits, wanted no more talk.

A few called out to Matheson to begin cutting. He obliged by selecting a razor from his array of cutting implements laid out on a small table behind him, and then slicing at the wrappings on the mummy's chest. He encountered some resistance, but it wasn't long before he'd made a long vertical cut from collar bone to groin. Once this was accomplished, he began peeling away the outer layer of bandages. He'd just loosened another layer when several objects that appeared to be small stones were released from the wrappings and tumbled to the floor before bouncing off the edge of the stage. They were quickly snatched up by those closest to the stage. One man held his prize aloft and exclaimed, "It's a scarab!"

Matheson hesitated, looked from side to side with an odd expression I could not read, and then back to the mummy. As he continued his work, he uncovered pieces of papyrus upon which hieroglyphics had been written. These he declared were charms of protection and prayers to the gods. "A good sign!" he declared.

With a final forceful wrench, he tore away a layer of wrappings from the mummy's chest. There was a gasp from the audience as Matheson lifted up a magnificent pectoral of gold, lapis lazuli, and other semiprecious stones. After that, he uncovered an oval, dark green stone covered in hieroglyphs which he declared was a heart scarab, a symbol of the emergence from nothingness into new life.

"Now," said Matheson, "the last thing is to get a look at the face of this priest." He took a small scissors from the table and began to snip at the bandages encasing the head. Suddenly, a look of perplexity overcame his face; he stopped snipping.

"Ladies and gentlemen," he said. "It appears that this man's head was cut off before he was mummified." He began cutting again. He made his cuts carefully over the face, and then pulled the bandages away in opposite directions. Suddenly, with a shout, he stepped back. The motion caused the table to rock, and the mummy's head rolled onto the stage where it lay staring at the audience. Lord Silverpin uttered a strangled cry. Startled, I turned to find Lord Silverpin and Lady Vivienne transfixed, staring at the grisly sight with looks of horrified disbelief on their handsome faces. Upon closer scrutiny, I soon understood why. Though desiccated and grossly deformed, the head that lay upon the stage was that of the Fifth Earl of Convarran.

After a brief pause, the audience, under the misapprehension that the performance had concluded, erupted with enthusiastic applause. Rising from their seats, they milled about, chattering, and laughing, as they moved to the front of the lecture room to get a closer look at the mummy's head. They had no idea that the body revealed when the mummy wrappings were unrolled was not the corpse of a three-thousand-year-old priest, but that of one of their contemporaries.

Matheson paid no attention. He was staring at the back of the lecture room with what appeared to be a look of profound incredulity upon his features. I turned to see what had captured his attention, I observed nothing unusual and returned my attention to the stage. In those few seconds, Matheson had vanished.

I cast about for Holmes, but he had not returned. Suddenly struck by the realization that I had become so caught up in the spectacle before me that I had forgotten about the Silverpins, now, stinging with shame, I turned my attention to helping them. They had been seated right beside me, but they were not there now. As I searched for them amid the mass of people, it was with disbelief that I found they had climbed onto the stage, picked up the Earl's head, and placed it near his body. They were standing guard, fending off people from the audience who were trying to get a closer look at the mummy. As I hurried to them, Lord Silverpin called out to me, "Fetch the police, Doctor! For God's sake, fetch the police!"

I needed no further urging. I turned on my heels and ran. As I passed into a corridor on my way to the street, I caught sight of Holmes racing in the opposite direction. I hesitated, torn between going after my friend or alerting the police. Then I thought of the Silverpins and the horror they were enduring and hurried on. Bursting through the great doors of the Egyptian Hall onto the street, it took me no time at all to locate a policeman. Breathlessly, I reported that a murder had been done inside. He jumped into action, blowing his whistle to summon more officers, one of whom he dispatched to Scotland Yard. I then led the constables back into the Egyptian Hall and to the lecture room where I had left the Silverpins. A few moments later, a blood-curdling scream stopped us in our tracks. Shaking off the shock, I clutched the arm of the constable nearest to me.

"Come! Come!" I cried, dragging him along.

When we finally entered the lecture room and he had surveyed the scene, he glared fiercely at me.

"What kind of prank is this?" he demanded. "You are reporting the murder of some old bundle of rags!"

"You don't understand," I explained. "You must recall that Lord Silverpin and Lady Vivienne reported their father, the Fifth Earl of Convarran, missing some two months ago. This mummy is the Earl. Someone has killed him and mummified his body."

The look of shock that came over the constable's face would have been comical had the situation not been so dire. It took him a moment, but then he became a whirlwind of action. He shouted for the audience to move away from the stage, followed by instructions to the two officers that followed him to detain everyone in attendance for questioning. I was quite impressed with this constable as our dealings with the police were often frustrating to say the least. It was often the case that the Scotland Yard detectives had better experience with crime scenes than the constables on the beat, who in the heat of the moment, often forgot or disregarded any training they might have received, if they'd had any at all, in dealing with such matters.

The Silverpins had covered the Earl with the purple velvet drape and continued to stand guard over their father's body.

Only now, with the constable taking charge, did I remember Holmes and the terrible scream I'd heard. I went to the Silverpins and told them I must find Holmes and that I would return as quickly as I could. I took my leave reluctantly for they both looked shattered. I hurried out into the passageway and turned in the direction where I'd seen Holmes.

As I progressed, I noticed an odor of smoke as well as something else, acrid and nauseating. It took a few moments for me to recognize the odor as burning flesh. I'd smelled it in Afghanistan; the combination of the smell and the recollection made me gag. I steadied myself against a wall for a few seconds before pressing on. I couldn't fathom what had happened that had produced the foul stench. There had been no cry of fire. It didn't take me long to discover it though. I came to a staging area at the back of the hall and my first sight was a group of people standing in a semi-circle. I recognized Inspector Crowe first. Then, I saw Holmes kneeling over a mound of smoking rubbish. Nearby, two policemen stood next to a man seated on a crate with his head in his hands.

"Holmes!" I cried. His head jerked around. When he saw it was I who had called him, he waved me over.

I hurried over and started to tell him that he was needed — that he and the others needed to come to the room where the Earl's body had been discovered. But the words died on my lips when I saw what Holmes and the others were looking at. It was Matheson, and there was no doubt he was dead. I recognized him, but just barely, for he'd been burned horribly and was for the most part a blackened mess.

"What has happened here?" I managed to get out.

Holmes said nothing, but Inspector Crowe extended his arm and opened his hand. In his palm, resting on his handkerchief lay a scarab identical to the ones that had been found in the Earl's study, on Sir Roger Trumbull's body, and in the bandages of the Fifth Earl's mummified remains. The fire had not damaged it in the least. It was almost too much to take in.

"I'm told you reported the murder," Inspector Crowe said. "Where did you get off to? We'll need your statement."

"I did report a murder," I said. "But not this one."

"What! There's been another?"

"Yes," I said. "The body of the Fifth Earl of Convarran has been found, though he's been dead for some time as you will soon see."

Inspector Crowe tucked the scarab into an inside pocket of his coat. "What in God's name are we dealing with here?" he asked.

Holmes turned shocked eyes upon me but said nothing. He stood and turned away from the grisly sight. He looked over at the man sitting on the crate. The poor fellow no longer held his head in his hands. Someone had made him a cup of tea and I saw one of his comrades pour something stronger into the cup.

"If I'm not mistaken," Holmes said softly, "that gentleman over there can give us some account of what happened."

"Then we'd best have a word with him," said Inspector Crowe.

The inspector, Holmes, and I approached the man upon whom a constable had been keeping a close eye. The man, an older gentleman, was one of the many employees of the Egyptian Hall who worked behind the scenes. He was dressed in an overall and clutched his mug of tea tightly with both hands. It was apparently his unfortunate lot to have been sent to fetch something from one of the staging areas when he heard a commotion and went to investigate. What befell him after that must have been quite traumatic as he was still pale and shaking from his ordeal. When he saw the three of us approaching, he started to rise, but a constable's hand on his shoulder pressed him back into his seat.

This unfortunate witness addressed Inspector Crowe with a quavering voice. "'ere now, I have naught to do with this business. I was about my work when it 'appened."

"I have no doubt that is true, Mr. …"

"Blough," the man said. "William Blough."

"You are a witness, Mr. Blough, our only witness by the looks of it. So, you must tell us what transpired here, everything that you heard and saw in as much detail as you are able."

"Leave nothing out," Holmes added. "It is sometimes the smallest detail that illuminates the darkness."

William Blough gave Holmes a look as if he thought him an odd bird, which perhaps he did. But another nudge from the constable started him telling his tale.

"Well, it was like this." He cleared his throat, and then drained his teacup before handing it off. "The guv'nor sent me back 'ere to search out some lumber for a platform that needs to be built for a magician's show as is coming 'ere next week. If we're late with them platforms and all else that must be done, well, we'll be scorched for sure."

"What was the time when you came back here?" Crowe asked.

"Well, I don't rightly know. I don't 'ave no watch of me own. Must've been some time past nine though, as that mummy show was beginning to wrap up."

Crowe recorded the time in his notebook. "What happened after that?"

"Well, I was lookin' for the wood. But I couldn't lay me 'ands on it. I got to thinkin' it must be in one a them far rooms. Things get shifted around 'ere regular like. It be the devil's own job to track a thing down sometimes. So, I starts back there when I 'ears someone shouting like."

"Shouting what?" Crowe asked.

"It weren't clear," Blough said. "It were loud and 'arsh sounding is all I can say."

"What did you do next?" Crowe asked.

"There weren't s'posed to be no one back there. Not at that time o' night. I went back there to see who it might be and what they was up to. We've 'ad some thieving recent, and the guv'nor is in a right lather to catch the buggers. Only now, I didn't 'ear no more shouting. Gone all silent, it 'ad. I thought maybe they 'ad a lookout and 'e seen me, and they'd scarpered before I could catch up with 'em. But then there comes this long, 'orrible scream. Stopped me in me tracks, it did. I wasn't going to go no further on me own, but then I smelled smoke and I 'ad to go on. If there was fire, I 'ad to try an' put it out and give the alarm."

Blough stopped then and took a deep breath. The constable patted his shoulder and told him to go ahead with his story. He looked down at his feet, then finally nodded and returned his gaze to us.

165

"I run in this room, then, and there was a fire all right. It were a man, still standing 'e was. I could see 'is eyes — they 'adn't melted yet, but that 'appened pretty quick. 'e was standing there one-minute burning like a torch and the next 'e was on the floor naught but a smoldering pile."

He shuddered, and then began rocking back and forth. He asked for a drink to steady his nerves and one of the constables went and presumably found someone with a flask willing to share for he returned in a few moments and filled Mr. Blough's teacup to the brim.

Crowe waited until Blough had drunk half his cup before asking if the victim had been alone.

Blough looked hard at Crowe. His eyes were those of a man unable to stop seeing the horror he'd witnessed.

"That's not the worst of it," he said quietly as he glanced about him as if he expected someone watching him. "There was another man. At least I thought 'twere a man. But when 'e turned toward me, I saw it weren't no man, but one a them mummies, only it was out o' its bandages and dressed like one a them pharaohs. 'orrible to look upon, it was." He turned his face away and it took a few moments for him to collect himself. He took another sip from his cup and swallowed hard.

"It were a dried up 'usk of a thing. But the eyes were the 'orror. I thought me 'eart would stop when it looked at me. Then somethin' struck me face. What it were, I couldn't say. I don't recollect nothing after that."

"This man, where did he go?" Crowe asked.

Blough shook his head.

"I don't know, sir. What I told you is all I know, and I wish to God, I didn't know it. After that thing looked at me, I was dead to the world until this constable 'ere lifted me off the floor."

We had all been mesmerized by Blough's fantastic story, but now my thoughts returned to the Silverpins.

"Good lord," I cried. "Holmes! The Silverpins. You must come at once!"

Chapter Seventeen

I had instructions to escort the Silverpins back to Mayfair and to stay with them until Holmes and Inspector Crowe could join us. We emerged from the Egyptian Hall to find the street crowded with theatregoers and gawkers who, attracted by the police whistles, were craning their necks whenever someone entered or exited the building. As I led the Silverpins through the throng, scanning the road for our carriage, I overheard snatches of conversations — people speculating on what drama might be going on within. While thus engaged, I was not immediately aware of a commotion gathering around us until Lady Vivienne screamed. I spun around to find that three swarthy men had laid hold of the Silverpins, attempting to drag them into the swirling crowd moving along the road.

One of the villains had grabbed Lady Vivienne. The other two grappled with Lord Silverpin. Lady Vivienne put up a magnificent struggle, clawing at the man's face, kicking at his legs, and biting his hands as he attempted to cover her mouth, but her attacker was a giant brute of a man and had little trouble overwhelming her. I shouted for the police as loudly as I could, hoping to be heard above the noise of the crowd, before wading in with my stick. I gave one of the blackguards accosting Lord Silverpin a fierce blow across his neck and shoulders. He shouted at the pain, releasing Lord Silverpin's sword arm. The young Lord did not miss a beat. Unsheathing his sword stick in an instant, he spun right and left, slashing at the men. From the villains' howls, I knew steel had met flesh.

I, in turn, pulled out my revolver and dashed after the brute forcing Lady Vivienne along the street. She had continued to struggle and shout for assistance to no avail. I could not fathom why not a single man attempted to intervene. Cowards the lot of them. The attacker was pushing her toward a coach parked at the curb. I could not shoot at him without endangering Lady Vivienne and other pedestrians, so I shot at the driver, sending a bullet whistling close by his head. That was enough to put horses and driver to flight. Lady Vivienne's assailant had grasped the door handle, but the force of it being yanked from his grip unbalanced him. Lord Silverpin had put to rout the two men who had accosted him and as they rushed past me, with the young lord in pursuit, they shoved me to the ground. All three now had Lady Vivienne in their clutches. Having lost one prize, it was clear they did not intend to lose the other. I struggled to stand while trying to ignore the pain in my leg. I could do no more than limp and I feared all was lost when I heard shouting behind me.

I turned to find people leaping out of the way of a carriage that was careening toward us at breakneck speed. As I stumbled out of the path of the charging horses, I looked up to see Jim Gladney, standing tall on the box, reins in one hand, whip raised in the other, bearing down upon our attackers like a juggernaut. The shrill of police whistles cut through the noise of the crowd. The constables were approaching with haste, and our attackers harkened to the sound. Such had been their focus on Lady Vivienne that they had failed to notice that Lord Silverpin and Jim Gladney had overtaken them. As I took in the scene unfolding before me, my breath caught in my throat and my heart thudded in horror at the catastrophe about to happen.

Before the villains could make another move, Lord Silverpin, running at full speed, flung himself bodily at his sister, wresting her from the thugs' grip. The two of them fell to the ground, clutching each other tightly, moments before Jim Gladney drove alongside the miscreants, furiously lashing his whip across their upturned faces. The constables now had our attackers in their sights and before they had recovered from young Jim's enraged assault, had them firmly in hand. I was much relieved to see that the Silverpins had rolled into the midst of passersby who were now gathered around the brother and sister, helping them to their feet and shouting for the police.

I saw Inspector Crowe shoving his way through the crowd of onlookers. No sooner had he reached me than he was hailed by a constable who came running over and whispered in his ear.

"Good lord," said the Inspector, "they have foxed us at every turn."

"What has happened?" I asked.

"Staunton has been attacked in his cell."

"What!" I cried. "How?"

"The police surgeon believes Staunton has been poisoned."

Chapter Eighteen

Holmes's plan had failed miserably. Three days had passed since the discovery of the Earl's body, Matheson's death, and the assaults upon the Silverpins and Staunton. We were both drained of energy. And far worse: We were beleaguered by melancholy and self-recrimination. Holmes's mood was so black we spoke little of what could be done next. But I knew, despite his mental anguish, my friend's great mind was busy parsing every aspect of the catastrophe. He slept and ate little, paced continually, and brusquely fended off any distraction to his concentration.

However, when an urgent telegram arrived from Inspector Crowe regarding Staunton, Holmes begrudgingly interrupted his contemplation to read it. Staunton had indeed been poisoned. Fortunately, he'd been discovered in time. The police surgeon had recognized the symptoms and was able to save him. This was a bittersweet victory, for Inspector Crowe had been unable to hold back Staunton's confession any longer and the experts in hypnotism consulted by Holmes and the inspector, while generally agreeing that Staunton was the victim of an assault upon his mind, had as yet been unable to fully explain the effects of that control, nor could they produce any other evidence that would help in his defense, let alone exonerate him. So it was that Staunton's confession and declaration of guilt had gone against him in the Crown Court. Due to the seriousness of the offenses — the murder of a peer

— and the stature of the victim, the trial was swift and the levying of justice even swifter.

It was this, the date of Staunton's execution, of which Inspector Crowe's telegram informed us.

"Surely," I cried, "the man is entitled to an appeal."

"He would have been had he not confessed and pleaded guilty," said Holmes as he folded the paper and slid it into the pocket of his dressing gown. "He did not try to save himself. Therefore, in the eyes of the law, he sealed his fate."

"Holmes! You cannot allow this miscarriage of justice. It's only been three days, let alone three weeks."

"Watson, there are limits to what even I can do. I have spoken on his behalf. We have brought forth expert witnesses to testify to his condition. It was not enough! There was not enough time!"

"My God," I said. My head was spinning with the news. "When is his execution to take place?"

"This very afternoon," Holmes said. "In fact, we had best attire ourselves and be on our way or we shall be late."

"Late," I gasped. Looking at the clock, I saw it was eleven o'clock.

"Staunton will be hanged at noon. If we are to offer him any succor, we must make haste."

I stumbled to my room, my brain in a fog. Surely this could not be happening. Perhaps on the high seas, in war, or among mercenaries such expedient executions occurred, but not in London in 1890, not in Her Majesty's England!

I have no memory of the hansom ride to Newgate Prison. Only that everywhere mists were rising beneath a lowering sky, and that even the lap rugs we spread across our knees could not deflect the cold's sharp bite. When we arrived before the prison gates, I saw the Silverpins' coach with Jim Gladney on the box turning in ahead of us.

Once inside, we joined Inspector Crowe and the Silverpins. Our passage through the halls of that grim gaol is a blur to me. My only recollection is that each way we traversed was darker and dingier than the last until we came to a sullen courtyard in which a gallows had been erected. Lady Vivienne gasped when she saw it. Jim Gladney paled and stood behind his employers, averting his eyes, no doubt experiencing pangs of guilt for the part he played in Staunton's fate.

Holmes and Inspector Crowe moved to the base of the platform where they observed two men, whom I presumed to be the warden and the executioner, as they prepared the gallows for its unfortunate victim. I saw Crowe nod in the direction of a building on the opposite side of the enclosure. I turned to see what they were observing. There at a window stood Staunton, another man beside him that I identified as a priest. Suddenly, a sharp bang broke the silence. The trap door in the gallows had banged open and a sack roughly the shape and weight of the condemned man plummeted through the hole. When I looked back to the window, Staunton had turned away; supported by the priest and a guard.

Lord Silverpin stared blankly at the gallows as if in a daze. He held his sister, her face turned away from the terrible sight and pressed tightly against her brother's chest. Jim

Gladney covered his face with his hands. From the rise and fall of his back, there was little doubt he was weeping.

The door to the building where I'd observed Staunton opened and two guards, one on either side of the coachman, walked him to the gallows with the priest following behind. If he experienced terror as to his fate, he did not show it. His features were stoic. As the guards walked him up the short stairs to the platform his knees gave way for a moment and the guards had to support him, but he recovered himself and went the rest of the way without weakness. As he turned to face the noose, he said something to the warden. The warden nodded and Staunton addressed the Silverpins.

"My Lord and Lady," said he, "I bore the Earl no animosity, yet I delivered him to his death, of that, I am sure. I am not mad. More's the pity, for if I were mad, I would have a reason to beg your forgiveness. As it is, I must go to my grave a dishonored man. All I can offer you is that I am sincerely sorry for what I have done. May God forgive me!"

What followed remains seared in my mind. The executioner placed the hood over Staunton's head, the priest said a prayer, the warden nodded, and the platform fell.

Chapter Nineteen

We arrived at the Diogenes Club on Pall Mall across from St. James Square where we were to meet Holmes's older brother, Mycroft. The area was home to many prestigious clubs and hotels, and adjacent to the government offices at Whitehall. Holmes reminded me that once we had crossed the threshold, we must maintain utter silence until ushered into the Strangers Room, the only place within the club's precincts where conversation was allowed. Most men's clubs in London encouraged fellowship and conviviality among members. That the Diogenes Club did not encourage congeniality was both peculiar and unique. I had remarked on this in the past and I said as much again.

"The Diogenes Club was not founded for the average man, or even the exceptional man," Holmes explained with an air of impatience. "The men who are members of the Diogenes Club have one commonality: they are misanthropes one and all. They have no need of, nor desire for, the company of other men."

"What about women?" I asked mischievously. "Surely, some of these men have families."

"I daresay, most are quite content to keep their own company," replied Holmes with a sidelong glance, "though it is possible that a few are married."

"Has your brother no desire to marry?"

"He does not. The Queen's business keeps him sufficiently occupied. It would be a serious impediment to his work if he were encumbered with the responsibilities that come with a wife and children, let alone a household, and social obligations."

Despite my long association with Sherlock Holmes, I knew little of his brother, Mycroft, although, the more I learned of him, the more I found him to be a good deal like my friend.

"Well," I said. "At any rate, I hope you give him a piece of your mind. What cheek, recommending you to the Silverpins and then advising them to withhold information."

"Quite." Holmes's attempt at a smile was strained and appeared as more of a grimace. "Like any government official, he is compelled to take control or believe that he has."

The front entrance to the Diogenes Club was no more than a stone's throw from its famed neighbor the Carlton, a small, nondescript brass plaque its only means of identification. We passed through its doors into a simple but elegant hall tastefully appointed with oriental runners and Chinese pots filled with large, luxuriant ferns. The only furnishing, a curved-legged, lacquered writing desk guarding the entrance to the members' only rooms, was presently unoccupied. A placard informed visitors that absolute silence must be maintained at all times, and in the absence of an attendant one should ring for assistance. Within seconds of Holmes employing the bell, a door opened on the opposite side of the hall and a middle-aged man dressed in butler's kit emerged. He bowed deferentially before silently directing us into the Strangers' Room where we found Holmes's brother ensconced in an over-sized, over-stuffed armchair, awaiting our arrival and observing us through heavy-lidded eyes.

The attendant, having been immediately issued an order for refreshments, bowed and took his leave. When the door had closed behind him, Mycroft Holmes rose with some effort and my friend stepped forward.

"I am sure you recall my friend and colleague, Dr. Watson."

"It is a pleasure to see you again, sir." I shook his hand, which nearly engulfed my own, and found it as soft as a baby's yet with an astonishingly strong grip.

"And you, Doctor," said he. "Sherlock speaks highly of you at every opportunity."

Mycroft Holmes was a big man, both rotund and tall. His nose was prominent and quite noticeably crooked. I wondered if its appearance was natural or if it had been broken at some time and not properly set. His hair, while fashionably cut, was untidy. His fingers were stained with ink and some brown substance and could have done with a good scrub.

At his invitation, we settled into a pair of deep leather chairs before a warming fire, after which he offered us some fine Egyptian cigarettes. Holmes and I each took one, exclaiming upon the pleasing fragrance. Our host did not partake, but instead removed from his waistcoat pocket a small, gold, enameled box from which he extracted and then inhaled a measure of snuff.

There came a light tap at the door followed by the attendant who entered with a tray of drinks which he set upon the table and immediately took his leave.

Holmes the younger lifted a glass, took a sip of whiskey, and nodded appreciatively. "I presume you heard about the incident at the Egyptian Hall?" said he.

Mycroft grunted. "It is in all the papers. If you had come to me when I first summoned you, such perverse drama would have been avoided."

"Indeed, it could have been if you had not advised the Silverpins to withhold information from me," my friend replied tartly.

Mycroft bared his teeth in a rictus smile. "I knew you would summarily refuse any case with even a faint whiff of the occult. However, if, while investigating this unusual abduction, you discovered such information, you would pursue it obsessively like a terrier after a rat. You might make noises about abandoning the case. But, at that point you'd be hooked. You would stay the course if for no other reason than to prove the folly of it."

"The Silverpins engaged me to find their father, nothing more."

"And you did so."

"I failed to find the Earl alive."

"The Earl was dead before you ever became involved. Surely, you've deduced that."

"Finding his killer will be some small amount of justice for my clients."

"You and I both know it to be Emm."

"Of course, but I cannot prove it. His house has been under surveillance round the clock, but I have been unable to lay my hands upon him. After the events at the Egyptian Hall, I sense another actor upon the stage."

"Emm attracted the attention of someone infinitely more powerful than himself who is after the artifacts for other than occult purposes."

I could hold my tongue no longer. "You talk as if the deaths of three men are unimportant!"

"Hardly, Doctor," said Mycroft. "But as you both must have realized by now, this case has never been about the Earl."

I gaped at the man. Surely, he could not mean what he had said.

"If you were only interested in the stone and the papyrus, why involve me at all?" snapped my friend. "Surely, with all your superior resources, you could have acquired them on your own."

"The Silverpins are reluctant to give them up. They had to be shown the danger they were in. With you on the case, I could be reasonably certain no harm would come to them in the process," said Mycroft.

Holmes grunted derisively. "You attempted to get hold of the artifacts yourself and failed."

Mycroft colored but his tone did not change. "Indeed," said he. "I did not anticipate such resourcefulness on the part of the Silverpins. I'm considering recruiting them for service to our government."

Holmes's eyes narrowed. "The urgent messenger for Lord Silverpin the day we arrived at Highmount was your man.

I suspected as much. But the watchers were either employed by Emm or this other actor."

"Emm is quite a skilled hypnotist, I'm told," said Mycroft evasively.

"You know of him?"

"Oh my, yes. I am astounded that you do not. He is a notorious scoundrel. Decent people will have nothing to do with him. He's been accused of indecency and deviancy any number of times. Though, I dare say, some consort with him secretly. He's invented his own religion, you know. At least he calls it such, though I'd wager upon examination you would find it closer to a cult."

"Why has he not been arrested?" I asked.

"He knows things about important people, Doctor, people whose reputations would be ruined if that knowledge were to be made public."

Holmes stubbed out his cigarette. Mycroft offered him another. He took it and, fetching a match box from his pocket, lit it. Leaning back in his chair, he exhaled a cloud of smoke.

"The watchers attempted to gain entry to Highmount House," said Holmes. "They were thwarted by the Silverpins and their servants, resulting in the death of their butler. It was one of these marauders who attacked me. They then attempted to abduct the Silverpins at the Egyptian Hall. But they were not the ones who killed Matheson. Of these two malefactors, one is bent on revenge above all else, and the other is after the artifacts for his own purposes."

"These artifacts, as you call them, are extraterrestrial objects. If the rumors surrounding them are to be believed, they have the ability to create a gateway that could allow an alien race access to our world," said Mycroft.

"Rubbish! You no more believe that than I do, brother."

"Have a care, Sherlock. Ever since Euphonius Slate's stars beacon experiments, there has existed a secret branch of the government that investigates such possible threats."

"What is this stars beacon that you speak of?"

"As I am sure you are aware, the existence of extraterrestrial beings is debated from the Royal Court to the meanest rooms of Whitechapel. Professor Slate, a genius and inventor of the first order, took a notion to try to communicate with these extraterrestrial beings. To that end, he created a machine that would send a repeating signal into space. To his astonishment, as well as ours, they, whoever they are, replied."

"What?" I cried. "You can't be serious!"

"I am completely serious, Doctor. Our imagination both frees us and constrains us. What if these things are beyond what we can imagine? If there are portals to other universes and those doors are opened, we have no way of knowing who or what may come through them. It is true, we do not know if there is any accuracy in these rumors, but if there is even a grain of truth in them, it is a perilous threat to the Empire if they fall into enemy hands. We believe these artifacts could be a potential weapon and that this unknown actor means to obtain them to use or sell to the highest bidder. We are in the midst of the Great Game. One hears whispers of war everywhere."

Holmes sat ramrod straight and rigid in his chair.

"The Silverpins could surrender the artifacts to these criminals or to you and be free of this persecution," Holmes declared. "But they do not. Why? Because they fear the intentions of their pursuers and they do not trust you. They believe that all parties will use these artifacts for ill."

Mycroft bristled. "You know me better than that," said he, his voice tinged with reproach. "The Silverpins are rational people, but the woman, Neferuptah, who I understand is their mother, has influenced them unduly. I think you will find, brother, that she believes her son, Lord Silverpin, to be a descendant of an ancient line of God-Kings, to be a pharaoh himself. Those radicals who call themselves the Protectors of the God-Kings are her men. She has been cultivating these ancient beliefs in her children from the time they were babes in arms. She believes they are destined to do battle with this corruption, as she calls it, and destroy it, if that is even possible."

"You are very well-informed," said Holmes.

"Well," said Mycroft. "There's only one man to whom one can turn for information on such matters."

My friend's face darkened. "Scarabus."

"Who else? You are not so naïve as to think that you are the only person involved in this matter to have consulted him. And, assuredly, you would be a fool to think he is not playing his own game as well."

Holmes gave his brother a sharp look. "I have had Scarabus under surveillance. I have seen with my own eyes his meeting with a man who may very well be Emm or this other unknown party who acts from the shadows."

"We are aware of the Watchers," Mycroft continued. He took a deep drink from his glass while staring out the window onto Pall Mall, perhaps weighing what he would say next. "We captured one, an Egyptian, but we could get nothing from him."

"Where is he now?" my friend asked.

"Dead."

"How?"

"Not our doing."

"Who then?"

"By his own volition; he tore open a vein with his teeth and bled to death."

The grotesqueness of the image caused me to shudder. "Good lord," I whispered.

"We believe," said Mycroft "that he and his countrymen followed Emm out of Egypt in order to recover the artifacts Emm had stolen from them. I believe we have rounded up the lot of them. They are no longer a threat to your clients."

"There is still the matter of justice for the Earl and the Silverpins. You will recall the matter about which I wired you yesterday."

Mycroft frowned. "Very well, you shall hear from me shortly. I remind you that in this matter, your duty is to Queen and country. The government must not be involved in the acquisition of the artifacts. Is that understood?"

"Quite."

And with that, Mycroft Holmes dismissed us with a wave of his hand.

As we took our leave, Mycroft, a sardonic smile playing over his lips, called after my friend.

"Sherlock, I trust that I have impressed upon you the enormity of the situation and that you need no further instruction from me on the need for expediency and discretion in this matter."

Without another word, a stony-faced Holmes grasped my arm and propelled me through the door.

Chapter Twenty

After our contentious meeting with Mycroft Holmes, we hailed a cab and set off for Baker Street. I was uneasy during the whole of our journey for Holmes, his thin lips drawn tight in a grim line, spoke not a word nor could I draw him out. Any attempt at discourse was met with a grunt, a steely look, and impenetrable silence. I was all too familiar with this behavior. My friend was slipping into a black funk, a dark malaise that would, I feared, soon prostrate him or worse — drive him to the cocaine bottle. The deaths of the Earl, Matheson, and Staunton, the assault upon the Silverpins, his failure to capture Emm at the Egyptian Hall, and his brother's startling revelations and harsh criticism had wounded him and, though he would never admit as much, caused him to doubt his methods and his actions.

Upon our arrival at 221 B, we met Mrs. Hudson at the door, she having just collected the post.

"Your post, Mr. Holmes," said she with a smile and outstretched hand.

Holmes brushed past, dismissing her with a wave of his stick as he ascended the stairs.

"Well, I never," said she, staring daggers at his back and vibrating with indignation.

Our landlady, whose demeanor was typically gentle and imperturbable, was nevertheless a born and bred Scotswoman and could be incited to high temper by such discourteous behavior. I moved quickly to intervene, taking her arm, turning her away from the stair, and whispering in her ear that Holmes was not himself, and assuring her that I would come down later and explain all. Somewhat mollified, she thrust the correspondence into my hands and retreated to her sitting room, shutting the door firmly behind herself.

When I reached our rooms, Holmes had already disappeared into his bedchamber. I found his overcoat, hat, stick, and gloves discarded upon the floor and to my dismay the center drawer of his desk open and his syringe case missing. After hanging up our coats and hats, I perused the post. There were a few letters and telegrams whose senders I did not recognize, and a small parcel from Inspector Crowe. I placed the letters and telegrams on Holmes's desk, then went to his door and knocked. Receiving no response, I knocked again, and then tried the knob. The door was locked.

"Holmes, there is a parcel here from Inspector Crowe," I called through the door. There was only silence from within. Sighing, I said, "I'll put it with the other correspondence on your desk."

I dropped the package on the desk then went to the sideboard and poured myself a whisky. I drank it in one swallow, then poured and drank another. In the whole of my association with Holmes, I had never known his plans to fail in such a spectacular fashion. The death of one of his clients in the previous year had already been preying upon his mind. I could only imagine the anguish the deaths of three more innocents would heap upon his soul. There was nothing more I could do for my friend but let him lick his wounds in private and purge his mind of self-recrimination by his preferred method. As for myself, I had no desire to be alone with my misgivings. I poured a third whisky and drank it with less haste before taking myself downstairs where I hoped to prevail upon Mrs. Hudson's good nature to share her table and spend the evening in her company.

The next morning, I tiptoed down the stairs and peeped into our sitting room. Holmes, wrapped in his mouse-colored dressing gown, was sprawled upon the settee, his Stradivarius abandoned on the floor beside him. I had dreamed, or so I thought, that I heard him playing in the night. Though I was careful to make no noise, Holmes spoke to me without turning his head.

"Come in, Watson. I shan't bite."

The man had the hearing of a bat. I ventured into the room, observing him closely for signs that he had once again succumbed to his practice of self-poisoning. He was pale, with dark stains beneath his eyes. He appeared to have abandoned his usual fastidiousness for his hair was uncombed and his face unshaven.

He gazed at me with somber eyes. "If ever a man has so thoroughly misread every clue put before him, Watson, I am that man."

"Surely not, Holmes."

"I've been a fool. And worse, I have failed to perceive the larger picture. The evidence is everywhere, but I allowed my prejudice to blind me."

"What is it that you have missed, tell me," I said. "I do not see how you could have acted differently."

"What I have missed, Watson, is that Moriarty is behind it all!"

"Professor Moriarty!" I cried.

"Yes, Watson, Professor Moriarty. Do you not recall what Madame Neferuptah said? The papyrus shows a mathematical formula that creates a portal to other dimensions, other places in time and space. The stone is both a beacon and a conduit into our world. What a man such as Moriarty could do with that knowledge. It is inconceivable!"

"Holmes, you astound me. Are you now giving credence to this fairy tale?"

"Think man!" cried Holmes springing up from the settee. "These objects are not magical nor are they the bearers of an ancient curse or even objects of superstition. That is the fairy tale. They are something else, incredibly old, and yet altogether new. These objects are not of this world."

"Holmes, I don't understand what you're talking about."

He paced furiously to and fro, gesticulating, a sheen of perspiration upon his face.

"Why do you think so many seek to obtain them by any means? Subterfuge! Violence! Murder! And why do others seek to destroy them with equal passion? If these objects have the powers attributed to them and Moriarty were to lay his hands upon them, he could hold all of England in his thrall, perhaps even the world. There is no end to the evil that might be wrought if one had such power. Why do you think Mycroft is hell-bent on obtaining them for the government?"

"Holmes, this is too much! It's poppycock! Preposterous!"

"You would not say so if you had spent the night with this, as I have," said Holmes. He reached into a pocket of his dressing gown and withdrew a small object that he gripped tightly in his fist. Slowly, he stretched out his hand and let his fingers unfurl. In the palm of his hand lay a scarab.

I recoiled at the sight of it.

"When did you get this?" I cried. "Everywhere these scarabs have appeared men have died."

"Calm yourself, Watson, Inspector Crowe sent it along in yesterday's post," Holmes replied.

It occurred to me that Holmes's exposure to the scarab for an extended period, in combination with the effects of the cocaine, would account for his unhealthy appearance and febrile state.

"What did you experience?" I asked.

"When we first encountered these scarabs, I did not tell you truthfully what I experienced. I felt a surge of energy so powerful, for a moment it made me quite giddy. I felt … I felt as if no power on Earth could constrain me. Last night, I experienced the same sensation and also as if something were there, on the other side of a door, so to speak, a presence, listening, waiting, as if for an invitation. All the while the scarab glowed green with phosphorescence. I felt my mind, nay, dare I say it, my entire being drawn by this power. There was nothing I could do to thwart it until at the last my mind rebelled, and a force — I can think of no other way to describe it — came forth from within me and tore me away from that malignant stimulus. I felt limp as a rag, as if I had struggled mightily with a superhuman opponent. Then I recalled what Madame Neferuptah said. 'Light repels it.' I lit all the lamps and subjected the scarab to the full glare of light. How the thing howled, Watson. I could hear it in my mind, and then I felt it withdraw. Yet, even now, in its weakened state, it exerts its force upon me."

Holmes strode to the window and placed the scarab upon the sill in the full light of the sun. His words had filled me with terror.

"Hallucinations, surely!" I cried. "Brought on by the effects of cocaine upon your unsettled mind."

He turned wild eyes upon me.

"All roads lead to Moriarty, Watson," he shouted. "You can depend upon it. He is the puppet master in this affair. And I have done nothing but dance to his tune."

I caught my friend by the arm and guided him to the settee. "You must rest," I implored. "You have pushed yourself too far. If you persist, I will have no recourse but to prescribe a sanatorium."

He shook me off and went to stand by the fire.

"No," said he. "Now is not the time for rest, but for action. This experience, this revelation, has turned my anguish to anger. I know what must be done. But I cannot do it alone."

Chapter Twenty-One

After taking sustenance and a few hours sleep, Holmes recovered himself and spent the remainder of the day in communication with various parties he had enlisted to plan the next assault upon our enemies. I had intended to lose myself in a book, but I couldn't prevent my thoughts from replaying the dreadful events at the Egyptian Hall and Newgate Prison. Now, we sat by the fire sipping warm brandy. The calming effect was welcome as my nerves were still raw. Without hesitation, I filled my glass a third time with a full measure of brandy. Holmes stared into the flames. I couldn't tell if he was absorbed in thought, or like me, attempting to forget for a time the events of the past few days.

"Holmes?"

"Yes, Watson."

"You've been engaged in a council of war all this afternoon. Will you not tell me our next move?"

"We shall bait the trap again with an offer our adversary cannot refuse. And this time, he will not slip through our fingers."

This was said with no little resentment. The tragedy at the Egyptian Hall had added insult to the guilt my friend was already feeling by castigating himself for his failure to foresee the future. Personally, I didn't see how anyone could have imagined the events of that night and I said so. But it did no good.

"We will take him at Highmount House. The Silverpins, Madame Neferuptah, and Inspector Crowe will all play their parts, and you and I, Watson, we shall be the vanguard."

"Can you not tell me more?"

"When we are all assembled at Highmount, all will be laid out."

"Really, Holmes, this is intolerable! How am I to assist you if I am always in the dark? If I do not have access to what you know, I am useless."

"Hardly, old boy, hardly," said Holmes, in what I considered to be an altogether too cheery tone. "By the by, did I mention I've had a telegram from Inspector Crowe?"

"No, Holmes. You neglected to tell me." I'm afraid I couldn't keep the irritation out of my voice. His insistence on secrecy and his attempt to change the subject made me quite peevish.

"Pray, do not keep me in the dark. What does he say?"

Holmes turned his gaze upon me, one eyebrow raised. "He says that Staunton's memory has returned. He now remembers who he transported to the train station the morning of Earl's disappearance. Unfortunately ..."

I sat bolt upright in my chair. My book slipped from my hands and clattered on the floor. "What?" I cried. "Staunton?"

"Calm yourself, old friend. Staunton lives. His hanging was a ruse. We had tried everything else to free him from the hypnotist's control. Our last resort was to expose his mind to so great a shock that it would reorder itself, so to speak. At least, that was the Viennese alienist's theory. Thanks to

Mycroft, Inspector Crowe, and Dr. Hyslop of Bethlehem Royal Hospital, we were successful."

I was beside myself. "Holmes, this is monstrous!"

"Needs must when the devil drives, Watson, and make no mistake, my friend, it is a devil with whom we contend."

"My God," I cried. "This is the worst possible situation. The poor man has endured an assault upon his reason, poisoning, hanging, and now the noose will surely be put around his neck again and this time it will not be a ruse as you call it!"

However dire the circumstances, what Holmes and the others had done was unconscionable. Worse, he had allowed the rest of us to believe that we were witnesses to the final agonizing moments of a man's life. I can hardly describe the outrage I felt, coupled with the conviction that I should remove myself from Holmes's orbit, refuse to be his satellite any longer. Without another word to Holmes, I leapt from my chair, snatched my overcoat, hat, and stick, and bolted from our rooms.

I flung myself out the front door, slamming it with such force it seemed the whole house quaked. I stood on the pavement shaking with anger. How dare Holmes perpetrate so grotesque a deception upon us? Did he believe us so far beneath him that we occasioned no more concern than an insect? I fought the urge to look up at our windows and the warm light that so often welcomed me home. Footsteps from within alerted me to Mrs. Hudson's approach, no doubt coming to see who was abusing her house. I hesitated a moment only, and then fled, driven by a fury that burned all other thoughts to ash.

I rushed past the few pedestrians I encountered taking no notice of them even, to my shame, ignoring a former patient who called out a greeting. I strode along blindly, oblivious to my surroundings.

As my energy began to wane and my pace slowed, I found myself unaware of how much time had passed or how far I had traveled. My breathing had become labored, and my injured leg throbbed ominously. I surveyed my surroundings. Darkened, dingy buildings loomed above me. The narrow street, filthy with icy sludge, offal, and horse dung, was empty of traffic. There was no sound other than a whispering breeze that swirled the yellow fog this way and that. I had no idea where I was. Unlike Holmes's encyclopedic knowledge of London, mine was minimal at best. Could I have traveled so far from Baker Street? My sense of direction, usually dependable, had all but deserted me. I felt a stab of panic as I struggled to get my bearings. It was the darkness, surely, and the fog, that rendered the landscape alien and unrecognizable. Upon closer inspection, it seemed I had entered a commercial district, an area of warehouses and industrial concerns inhabited during the day and all but abandoned at night. The meager light from the few streetlamps failed to illuminate any sign that might have given a clue to my location.

I had not felt the cold before, but I felt it now creeping in wherever it could. I turned up my collar, thrust my hands in my pockets, and stamped my feet. Further, in my rushed departure, I had forgotten my galoshes. I could feel the cold wet seeping into my boots. I thought of hailing a cab, but none was in sight and not likely to be in this wasteland.

I decided to retrace my steps as best I could. I needed to clear my mind and plan for the night. As I made my way back the way I'd come, I heard footsteps coming toward me, yet I could see no one. However, it was some little comfort to know I was not alone and that I might prevail upon the kindness of these strangers for directions. The footsteps sounded louder now. A few moments later, I was able to make out the forms of two men. As we drew closer together, they stepped apart one from the other, making it impossible for me to do other than pass between them. I shivered as a tremor of anxiety passed through me. Feeling foolish, I squared my shoulders, gripped my stick tightly, and hailed them.

"Hallo!" I shouted.

They did not answer my call but drew abreast of me in silence. They were a rough looking pair, laborers of some kind, no doubt. Holmes would have known their occupations with one look at their hands. The larger of the two gripped my arm.

"Lost are you, guv'nor?"

"Lost my bearings in this damnable fog," I answered, attempting to free myself.

In response, the ruffian tightened his grip upon my arm, twisting it cruelly. I raised my stick. At that moment, the other cur stepped behind me and struck the back of my head. My hat flew off, my stick dropped from my hand. I stumbled and fell to my knees. I did not lose consciousness entirely, yet I could not recover my faculties. Blood roared in my ears, my vision blurred and dimmed, the slightest movement triggered a stabbing pain in my skull. I sensed they were dragging me. Were we so far from humanity that there was no one to observe my plight and render assistance? I tried to regain my footing, but each time they kicked my legs from under me. I must have lost consciousness for a time. When I opened my eyes again, I could sense that we were near a thoroughfare, I could hear traffic and snatches of conversation.

I lay in a heap upon the freezing pavement. One of my attackers, his back propped against a wall, stood guard over me. We were concealed in shadows, so I had no difficulty maintaining a pretense of unconsciousness while I assessed my situation. My stick was gone, my clothing befouled, and I was still light-headed. Before I could conceive of any action, a brougham rattled to a stop in the street beside us. A man jumped down from the box, presumably my other attacker. The two thugs gripped me roughly under the arms and hauled me to my feet, dragging me to the four-wheeler. If they succeeded in their endeavor, all would be lost. I would be at their mercy. If I could but escape into the road, I could shout for a constable or beseech a fellow citizen for aid. They let loose of my arms as they attempted to shove me into the carriage. I balked, kicking, and shoving as best I could. I felt one of the men stumble and give way. A spark of hope strengthened my resolve and I swung about wildly with renewed energy. Unfortunately, the villain had climbed into the carriage. When I spun around to confront his comrade, he grabbed me from behind and dragged me inside. I cried out for help, but none came. My struggles were all in vain. I was again struck viciously upon the head and this time I was dead to the world.

Chapter Twenty-Two

I regained consciousness in an unfamiliar room, drab and sparsely furnished, an untended fire smoldering in the hearth. I was laid out upon a settee and to my surprise my limbs were not bound. The gas jets were turned down to flickers so much so that the room, except for my little area illuminated by the sputtering fire, was in shadows. I righted myself and attempted to rise when a deep, maleficent voice spoke from the shadows.

"Stay where you are, Doctor."

Startled, I fell back upon the settee. "Who are you?" I demanded as I sought the source of the voice. "What do you want with me?"

"My name is not important. As to what I want, only to help you. Were you not in the greatest distress when my men found you?"

"Your men are responsible for my distress." I was now aware of an awful throbbing behind my eyes. A cautious examination of my head revealed two lumps the size of hen's eggs. I could barely endure touching them. Despite the meager fire, I still felt the bite of the cold in my bones. My teeth chattered and I suffered bouts of uncontrollable shaking.

"I am fortunate not to have suffered a serious concussion from their violent treatment of me."

"They hadn't much choice," said my captor, "as you foolishly resisted their efforts to help you."

"Help me!" I cried. "They assaulted me."

There came a tap at a door I could not see.

"Come," said my captor.

One of my attackers entered bearing a tray. He set it upon a small table which he then positioned in front of me. He removed one plate from the tray and carried it into the shadows where he presumably delivered it to my host.

"Do not attempt heroics, Doctor Watson. Though you cannot see them, you are surrounded by my servants who will quickly subdue any action you might attempt against me and prevent your escape. Instead, fortify yourself with these victuals. You have had nothing to eat or drink since your abrupt departure from Baker Street."

"Oh, ho," I said, "Now it becomes clear. You are Professor Emm. It is your minions who have been watching our house. It is the only way you could know my movements."

"Perhaps," said he. "There will be time for talk later. Eat now, before your meal becomes cold and unpalatable."

I examined the food that had been set before me. There was a bowl of stew, some buttered bread, and a pot of steaming tea. I had little appetite, but the fragrant aroma of the tea enticed me. I do not doubt my judgment was impaired. Perhaps if I had been in complete control of my faculties, I would have questioned the advisability of my actions. But as it was, I did not: I filled a cup and sipped it. I managed a few mouthfuls of stew and a bite or two of bread. I could stand no more as my stomach remained queasy from the assault upon my skull.

Somewhere in the shadows, I heard cutlery clinking against crockery. A short time later, at a sign from my host, the dishes were cleared away.

"I demand you release me," I said.

My host chuckled. "You are hardly in a position to make demands, Doctor. Do not exert yourself; I will release you after you have answered my questions."

"What manner of questions?"

"Do not be coy, Doctor. It does not suit you. As I am sure you have already surmised, I desire information about the Silverpins, Sherlock Holmes, and the Egyptian artifacts that were stolen from me."

So, we had come to it at last. I had no one to blame but myself. My impetuous escape had placed me in this predicament. A horrible certainty settled over me that I had irreparably queered Holmes's investigation. I could not quell the anxiety which rose within me for, as Holmes's assistant, I had seen first-hand what men implacably bent upon an object would do to any that stood in their path. Ruination. Torture. Murder. They brooked no opposition to their desires.

"You may do your worst. I will tell you nothing." I said this with a great deal more conviction and bravado than I felt. In truth, my bowels had turned to water and my heart was racing. I could feel a cold sweat seeping from my skin.

"There is no need for such melodrama, Doctor. However, I will advise you that your cooperation now will save you untold distress in the near future."

"I will not be moved." As I spoke, I felt a slight giddiness and then such a wave of euphoria washed over me, I was unable to prevent myself from giggling.

"Ah," said my host. "It begins."

"What is happening?" I said with alarm, for I was quickly becoming detached from my body. "Fiend!" I cried, "You have drugged me."

A figure emerged from the shadows and took a seat facing me. I struggled to focus on his countenance, but his features were in constant motion, bending and twisting. I became dizzy with the effort. He held a medallion before my eyes. It spun slowly, its many facets sparkling like brilliant stars. So arresting was it, I could see nothing else. His voice, previously harsh and menacing, now seemed like ambrosia to my ears as he urged me to relax and sleep. Sleep is what I needed, yes, more than anything, sleep, and as I succumbed to his ministrations he said:

"Now, Doctor, let us begin. Tell me, where are the Egyptian artifacts?"

Chapter Twenty-Three

I awoke to Holmes, Mrs. Hudson, and Inspector Crowe standing over me with looks of the utmost concern upon their faces.

"Holmes ..." I murmured.

"Don't trouble yourself, old friend; you're back at Baker Street in your own bed. We've had the police surgeon in to examine you and he assures us that with rest and sustenance you will be right as rain in no time."

"Rest now, Doctor," said Inspector Crowe. "You've been through quite an ordeal."

I gazed upon my friends in utter confusion. "What has happened?" I asked.

The three exchanged glances. Holmes sat on the edge of my bed. Inspector Crowe drew up a chair. I thought I saw Mrs. Hudson brush away a tear before she declared we all needed a strong cup of tea and bustled off to fetch it.

"Do you not remember?" Holmes asked. "Two nights ago, you stormed out in a frightful temper. Fortunately, Wiggins was on watch. He was startled by your hasty departure and was torn whether to stay at his post or follow you. The decision was made for him when he observed our lurker emerge from the shadows and hot foot it after you. Wiggins followed him, saw him meet up with another man, and witnessed your abduction. He stuck with you until he knew where they'd taken you and then he rushed back here and alerted me to your circumstances."

"My abduction?"

"Mr. Holmes came blazing into the Yard," continued Inspector Crowe, "and together he and I and a brace of constables went to the address reported by young Wiggins and surrounded the place. Unfortunately, by the time we arrived, they had gotten the wind up and cleared off, taking you with them."

"We had no idea of your fate," said Holmes "until a constable found you unconscious in an alley near the St. Marylebone Workhouse. You were taken to Middlesex Hospital where, fortuitously, one of the doctors recognized you."

While Holmes and the inspector were relating all this to me, Mrs. Hudson reappeared with a tea tray. Inspector Crowe gave up his seat and went in search of another. When he returned, he accepted a cup, and then turned his attention to me.

"What can you tell us, Doctor, about the men who abducted you?"

I was at a complete loss. Try as I might, I could recall nothing about the men Holmes and the inspector said had assaulted and abducted me. Gone for two days, found unconscious in an alley, taken to hospital? It was as if they were relating the adventures of some other person.

"I remember nothing about what you have described."

"What is the last thing you do remember, old boy?" Holmes asked. "Let's begin from there."

"Yes," said Inspector Crowe. "Going over what you do remember often aids in bringing to light what you do not."

What did I remember? When I was able to concentrate, fragments of memory flashed in my mind like sparkles of sunlight on dark water. I could make no sense of them. The sparkles were just that, minute flashes – a chipped brick, a smear of butter on a bit of bread, a carriage lamp – but I could not penetrate the dark depths beneath them.

Despite all their prompting, I could recall nothing substantial, and they finally gave it up. Holmes begged me to sleep and assured me everything would look better in the morning. I doubted his optimism, but my efforts had exhausted me, and I obliged without resistance. My last thoughts before I once again succumbed to sleep surprised me. They were of the Silverpins' coachman, Staunton, and Holmes, and that which had sent me flying from my friend. I struggled to press on and remember more, but in my weakened state it was impossible. If I could at least hold on to this knowledge until morning, perhaps I could remember more of the events of that night.

The morning found me in a quandary. After having recalled Holmes's deceit, I found my anger had cooled, but my sense of outrage had not. What was I to do? I could not bring myself to break from my friend, for while his actions had been monstrous, I knew him to be an honorable man, not a monster. But to go on without protest was impossible.

A short while later, I heard muffled conversation coming from our sitting room. Not long after that came a soft tap at my door, followed by Holmes bearing a breakfast tray.

My stomach harkened to the aroma of porridge and coffee, a good sign that I was on the mend.

"How are you feeling this morning?" he asked.

"Much better," I replied, maneuvering myself into a sitting position.

He looked at me expectantly, his keen gray eyes probing mine.

"Have you recalled anything?"

"Yes," I said. "I remember what caused me to flee from our home."

"Ah," said he. "I must apologize for subjecting you to such a shocking revelation. Sometimes my flair for the dramatic overpowers my common sense."

"I accept your apology," I said. "But, Holmes, I still must protest in the strongest possible terms your actions regarding Staunton and for all who witnessed this … this … atrocity. It is unconscionable. If this manner of deception should occur again, I'm afraid I shall have to end our association."

He regarded me thoughtfully.

"Lord Silverpin has connections in the very highest echelons of government, Watson. Testimonials from specialists and other experts, along with you and me, and the Silverpins themselves will no doubt secure a pardon. The campaign has already been set in motion. Staunton is no longer in police custody. He has been remanded to the care of Dr. Hyslop at Bethlehem Royal Hospital."

"Confinement in Bedlam is hardly an improvement!" I cried.

"He is not imprisoned there. He is receiving treatment and is an assistant of sorts to Dr. Hyslop. There was another reason for doing what we did, Watson. If the malefactor who compromised Staunton were to discover the mind-control with which he had ensnared him has been broken, Staunton's life would be forfeit. One attempt has already been made — you know this. With our plan we were able to free Staunton from that which subjugated him, get the information we need to apprehend and convict Emm, and make it appear that Staunton is dead, thus preventing further attempts on his life."

After listening to Holmes's explanation of what they had done to Staunton, I impressed upon him the deleterious aftereffects of traumatic shock and of the serious repercussions not only to Staunton but to the witnesses of Staunton's supposed execution.

Holmes gazed at me mournfully, then hung his head and sighed. "If anything else could have been done, Watson, I would have tried it. There was not. If I have caused injury, then I must live with the knowledge of the harm my actions have caused."

Though mollified, I now felt deflated, somewhat guilty, and perplexed at the dexterity with which Holmes had turned my condemnation into something akin to admiration. These words of Shakespeare came to mind: *"Cometh the hour, cometh the man."* As always, Sherlock Holmes was the man of the hour. He had not dithered. He had not hesitated. He had done what needed to be done regardless of the consequences, and in doing so had provided the only means by which Staunton's life might be saved.

We sat for a while in silence, each of us lost in our own thoughts. After a time, Holmes once again urged me to try to recollect what I experienced during my abduction. My inability to recall anything beyond my leaving 221 B was maddening. What had happened to me during that time? What had I done? What had been done to me? I could not escape the feeling that I had endangered all that Holmes had accomplished. But, confound it, if I could not throw light upon the past, at least I could make myself useful and throw all my energy into helping Holmes in the present.

"Holmes," said I, "what has happened with the Silverpins?"

"Ah," said he. "While you've been under the weather, we've been lying low and plotting. We are ready to bait and set the trap."

"I fear I have put your plans in jeopardy. I cannot explain it, but I feel it in my bones. But I beg you, do not leave me behind. You must allow me to help you, make amends, and set things right."

Holmes hesitated before answering. A shadow of some emotion I could not read passed over his features.

"You are not well enough …" he began.

"Holmes," I cried, "I am an old campaigner. I have endured much worse and persevered. I shall fight by your side in this struggle. I swear it. I will not be sent down."

A ghost of a smile touched his lips.

"I would have it no other way, old friend," said he.

Chapter Twenty-Four

Highmount House was dressed in mourning. And we, too, had donned black armbands and cravats. We were here because Holmes believed another assault upon the Silverpins was imminent. Still, our presence struck me as an intrusion. Our clients appeared both melancholy and exceedingly weary. We had gathered in the library, settled into deep leather chairs, pulled blankets over our knees, and gratefully sipped the brandy that Jessup brought us. For long minutes, we stared into the flames, each lost in his own thoughts, until Holmes broke the silence.

"Lord Silverpin and Lady Vivienne, I regret that it is necessary to intrude upon your grief, but there are urgent matters we must discuss, the primary being the apprehension of your father's killer and the killer of Sir Roger and Cedric Matheson, as well as the fate of the artifacts that caused this madness."

"You are quite right, Mr. Holmes," Lord Silverpin said. "Can you tell us now how our father came to meet his fate?"

Holmes set down his glass and contemplated for a moment the portrait of the Earl draped in black crepe that hung above the fireplace.

"Yes," said he. "I believe I have worked out the chain of events that led to your father's death. As you yourselves have ascertained from your father's journal, the seeds were sown in Egypt when your father, Trumbull, and Matheson determined to punish Emm by abandoning him in Cairo without documents or resources. Unfortunately, Matheson's outrage and temper got the better of him. Given the task of disposing of Emm, rather than abandoning him, he took him away somewhere and shot him, and as he stated, left him for the crocodiles. At first, I thought he was lying — Matheson would have known that crocodiles have not populated the Nile River from the Delta to Aswan for many decades. But then I recalled this was the very same conceit you used in the little stories with which you entertained Watson."

Lord Silverpin flushed, Lady Vivienne averted her eyes and smoothed the skirts of her mourning dress, but neither denied Holmes's accusation.

"As it was," Holmes continued, "Matheson believed he had killed Emm when in fact Emm had somehow survived being shot and followed his former compatriots back to England. He either knew or learned that your father had retained the artifacts and set about recovering them. He had not, I think, reckoned on your mother who knew the artifacts' history. I think he had also not bargained on other entities seeking to obtain the artifacts. I cannot prove it, but I suspect that Emm communicated with your father and when he could not strike a bargain with him, he resorted to more nefarious means — perhaps he even attempted to steal the artifacts. That is where Staunton comes into it. According to Jim Gladney your coachman began to display strange behavior a fortnight before you father's disappearance. We know now that was when Emm began conditioning Staunton with hypnosis. It was Staunton who assaulted the Earl in the underground chamber, he who sponged away the blood, and he who placed the Earl's body, unconscious, but alive, in the shipping crate that Emm transported to London."

"How did killing our father serve any purpose in recovering the artifacts?" Lord Silverpin asked, his voice tremulous with emotion.

"It served no purpose," Holmes replied. "Though I believe Emm's initial motive in kidnapping the Earl was to use him as a hostage to bargain with. The Earl was alive when he was concealed in the crate, but Emm's desire for revenge overpowered his desire for the artifacts. Something occurred; what that was we may never know for certain. The Earl was killed, and it was the Earl's death that set the rest of these actions into motion."

"Then you believe Professor Emm is behind all of this?" asked Lady Vivienne.

"Behind the murders, yes," said Holmes. "I have suspected so for some time. He has gone to ground. So, we must draw him out. However, Emm is not our only adversary. In the matter of the artifacts, I have identified no less than five other parties, including yourselves, whose intention it is to secure these objects for their own purposes. We cannot know when any of them may strike. But I fear it will be soon, and we must ensure we have the upper hand."

"Holmes!" I cried. "The message from Porlock! We are at war!"

"I'm glad the implication has finally dawned upon you, Watson. Now you understand our position."

Lord Silverpin shifted in his chair so that he faced Holmes. "Who are these other factions that you speak of vying for the artifacts, and who is this Porlock?"

"Porlock is a shadow, a whisper from the darkness, but I shall get to him and his part in this affair shortly. Let us look first at Professor Emm," said Holmes. "He is the original thief. He stole the artifacts for the esoteric power he believes they will bestow upon him. Next, are the watchers; they are Egyptians, a rival cult if you will. Emm trespassed upon their territory when he stole the artifacts. I believe that was the reason for the escalating assaults upon your father's expedition. This cult has tracked Emm and the artifacts to England with the object of repossessing them, by force if necessary. However, I do not believe we have any more to fear from them. I am informed that they have been captured and have destroyed themselves to a man. Then, of course, there is my brother, Mycroft. He is certain the legends reveal the true nature of the artifacts. It is his belief that, should any of the legends surrounding these objects prove to be factual, it could lead to an extraterrestrial invasion, or the artifacts could be used as a weapon. Should such a weapon fall into the wrong hands, it would pose a dire threat to the Empire — even to civilization. And finally, we come to Dr. Scarabus, the individual who binds all of these odd fellows together. Scarabus is an antiquarian of the first order and is the repository of much eldritch knowledge. He is a collector of a most inquisitive nature. I sought his counsel when we first encountered the scarabs, as did my brother, Mycroft, and you," Holmes said. "Wiggins and I became suspicious of his part in this affair when we observed him slipping away from your Mayfair residence through the tradesmen's door."

The Silverpins and I had been listening to Holmes with rapt attention.

"I can assure you, Mr. Holmes," said Lord Silverpin looking rather shame-faced, "our only purpose in securing the artifacts is to destroy them. They are evil. They corrupt all who touch them, unless the proper precautions are taken, and even then, they are dangerous. We wish justice for our father and the others, but they are dead. The greatest urgency now is the destruction of the artifacts."

"That is why you have been communicating with Dr. Scarabus?" asked Holmes.

"Yes," said Lord Silverpin. "But we see now that we have been deceived."

"What does this Scarabus want?" I asked.

"He craves what all such men crave, Watson — power, wealth, immortality."

Holmes paused for a moment to take a sip of brandy before addressing Lord Silverpin. "How do you plan to destroy the artifacts?"

"We are not sure," said Lord Silverpin. "We need more time. We know that bright light affects the stone, rendering it inert but not harmless. Whether prolonged exposure to intense light will destroy it, we do not know. We have tried to burn the papyrus, but it does not burn. These objects are not of this world, and they cannot be destroyed, at least by any ordinary means. We were counting upon Dr. Scarabus to advise us."

"Well," said Holmes. "We shall deal with him in due course. At present, he is not our chief worry."

There came a light tap at the door and our conversation ceased.

"Come," said Lord Silverpin.

A maid entered bearing a heavily laden tea tray which she deposited on a table close to our little group.

"Thank you, Starling," said Lord Silverpin.

The maid curtsied and made to depart. As she turned to the window her faced paled, her body became rigid, and she emitted a strangled cry. We all started at the sound.

"What the devil is the matter?" asked Lord Silverpin.

The girl turned, her face a mask of shock. "A face at the window, your Lordship. A face peerin' in."

"The watchers!" I cried. "They are still here!"

Lord Silverpin pulled a pistol from the pocket of his coat and he and Lady Vivienne, who also had drawn a weapon from the folds of her dress, ran to the window.

"Quickly, Watson," Holmes called. "Outside!"

As we bolted for the door, our progress was impeded by the butler, Jessup, who came through with a small boy in his grip. "Here is the culprit, my Lord," he said loosing his hold on the youngster's ear. "I have been observing this young miscreant sneaking about outside the house when I heard Starling cry out."

Lord Silverpin, looking quite relieved, nevertheless put on a stern face as he addressed the child.

"Tuppy isn't it?" he asked. "One of our stable boys."

The lad, obviously nervous, shifting from foot to foot, nodded.

"What were you doing peeking in at the window? Tell the truth now and you won't be punished."

Tuppy swallowed and cast a sidelong glance at Jessup and Starling who were hovering over him like vultures and who tutted at the suggestion that the boy would not be punished.

"I just want a see Mr. Sherlock Holmes," said Tuppy. "Jim told me all about his adventures and what he done up in London. I just want a see him."

Lord Silverpin had a hard time suppressing a smile. "Well, here he is, young man," he said indicating my friend.

"I'm pleased to make your acquaintance, Tuppy," said Holmes, offering the boy his hand.

Young Tuppy, with a bashful smile, shook Holmes's hand.

Lady Vivienne came over and handed Tuppy a half dozen sandwiches and tea cakes wrapped in a napkin. "You might have been mistaken for a burglar and come to harm," she said. "There will be no more sneaking about, do you promise?"

Tuppy, obviously in awe of the beautiful lady, nodded wordlessly as he clutched his prize close to his chest.

"Good," said Lady Vivienne. "Mr. Jessup, will walk you back to the stables."

"Where he shall stay and attend to his duties," declared Jessup as he placed his hand firmly on the back of Tuppy's neck and marched him out the door with the maid, Starling, close behind.

"Heavenly days," said Lord Silverpin after the butler, the maid, and the stable boy had left. "My heart is still racing."

We all murmured in agreement as we returned to our seats and tucked into our tea.

After he had eaten, Holmes stood and stretched, then walked to a world globe which he turned slowly.

"There is also a powerful, hidden force," said he, "that I did not at first perceive who can only be Professor Moriarty, a criminal mastermind who controls much, if not all, of the criminal activity in London. His motives are unclear, but you can be assured whatever his reason for coveting these artifacts, he will use them in service of his criminal network. Porlock — not his real name, of course — is a minion of Professor Moriarty who has upon a very few occasions informed me of his master's activities. The reasons for his intermittent involvement are unclear, but his intelligence has always proved reliable. Furthermore, unless I am very much mistaken, Emm will be paying you a visit. Now that he has had his revenge, he will be after the artifacts. It is not Moriarty's way to appear in person. He will be observing all the other players and will strike unseen when he sees his best chance. He is more suited to trickery and manipulation, as is, unfortunately, my brother. It is with all this in mind that I have devised a plan that shall set all these elements in motion, and you must be ready."

"Holmes!" I cried. "You can't be serious. You cannot put Lord Silverpin and Lady Vivienne at risk."

Lady Vivienne took her brother's hand in hers. "We are not afraid, Dr. Watson. In truth, we consider it our duty."

While the others continued to chat, I lit a cigarette, breathed in its aromatic scent, and listened to the cheery crackling of the fire in the hearth. The rhythmic ticking of a long case clock soothed my nerves, and I allowed my mind to drift over recent developments in the case. Prior to this conversation, I did not know what part the Silverpins and the others were to play, only that Lord Silverpin, Lady Vivienne, and Madame Neferuptah had been in deep discussion with Holmes. I was not privy to this, but I took no offense. With the culture and activities of the Osirans being secret, they had agreed to divulge only what was necessary and only to Holmes. I was now aware that Holmes had devised some grand scheme to lure Emm to Highmount, and if successful, we would take him into custody and turn him over to the police. How Holmes and Inspector Crowe intended to wrest a confession from him, I could not imagine. Outside of Staunton's testimony, we had no irrefutable proof that Emm had anything to do with the Earl's death, never mind the deaths of Trumbull and Matheson.

I understood that Holmes intended to send the Silverpins on a mission to convince Dr. Scarabus that they were seeking his help with the artifacts. During their consultation, they would appear to be convinced that the most sensible course of action was to turn the artifacts over to him for safekeeping. If successful, they would dispatch back to Highmount for the supposed purpose of returning to London with the artifacts after they had interred their father. Mycroft had bound Holmes to his duty to the Crown and therefore expected him to secure the artifacts for the government, thus ensuring that these two parties — Scarabus and Mycroft or his minions — would have no reason to make an appearance in pursuit of the stone and the papyrus.

With the Earl dead, the villains no longer had any leverage over the Silverpins, and since we had no way of knowing when Emm might strike, Holmes, intent on gaining the upper hand, advised Lord Silverpin to send a message to Emm's home stating that in view of the altered circumstances, they'd had a change of mind and heart and would part with the artifacts for a price. I had reminded Holmes that according to all our sources, Emm had no money, at least not the amount that the Silverpins would demand. "We shall see," is all he would say about the matter.

Not long after the message to Emm had been dispatched, Lord Silverpin received an unsigned telegram. Following Holmes's instructions, he rebuffed it, sending the messenger away with his only reply being that he would not treat with a man who refused to sign his name or show his face.

"Now that we know that Emm is in his house, should we not inform Inspector Crowe and avoid this confrontation?" I asked.

"We do not know that Emm is at his residence," replied Holmes. "We know that someone answered. It may be that those unsavory servants Lestrade spoke of delivered the message to him wherever he has gone to ground, or the message may have been intercepted by another party."

A second communication was received the following day. This time it was not a telegram but a handwritten message of a single word – AGREED – scrawled in a spidery script, the signature only an elaborately formed M.

"Well, well," said Holmes. "They are here already."

"They?"

"Surely, Watson, if it is Emm with whom we are communicating, you did not expect that he would come alone. It is entirely possible that whoever we face will try to take the artifacts by force. In fact, I expect it. I have put the word out that we have been dismissed by the Silverpins. Given our clients' purported change of mind, such an action would be a likely step on their part. Furthermore, the villains know that the Silverpins dare not inform the police. I am also counting on our adversary, in his arrogance, believing in the naiveté of our clients."

"He may not believe such a narrative."

"I do not expect him to, Watson. However, I can assure you he will come on the day and at the time that we demand."

To that end, Holmes and I, after attending the Earl's funeral, could be seen leaving Highmount in the Silverpins' coach. We were deposited at Whitchurch station and departed on a train bound for London. When we reached our destination, we disembarked into the milling crowds of Paddington. Holmes secured a cab which carried us at a brisk pace back to Baker Street. Before dismissing the cab, Holmes spoke a quiet word to our driver and pressed a generous tip into his hand. We hurried into the house rushing past a startled and protesting Mrs. Hudson. We left our long-suffering landlady befuddled, clutching a note Holmes had pressed into her hand as we sailed past her out the back door. We wended our way through gardens and alleys until we came out a few streets away where our cabbie waited. We clambered inside and pulled down the shades. He returned us to Paddington where we boarded a train back to Hampshire. We then traveled overland by cart and completed the remainder of the journey on foot under cover of darkness, returning to Highmount by way of the tunnel in the Chapel.

Holmes assured me that we were prepared for any possibility. I was not so certain. My hand slipped into my pocket and gripped my service revolver. A full box of ammunition rested in my other pocket. As Porlock had so succinctly stated, we were at war. I understood war.

Chapter Twenty-Five

In the cellars below Highmount House, the Fifth Earl of Convarran had constructed a replica of a pharaoh's mortuary temple. Indeed, the Earl, his body rewrapped in mummy's bandages, had been placed in an ornate sarcophagus and sealed in his burial chamber. Upon entering the Temple of the Osirans, we came down a wide corridor, its walls and ceiling completely covered with hieroglyphs and fantastic paintings. Both sides of the walkway were lined with life-size, painted statues of the Egyptian animal-headed gods – Anubis the Jackal, Bastet the Cat, Thoth the Ibis, Hathor the Cow, Horus the Falcon – and others I did not recognize. Animated by the flickering gaslight, they seemed to process along with us as we made our way to the ceremonial room.

Before we took up our positions, we stepped into the chamber where the artifacts were housed. The room was ablaze with light and in the center, beside a pedestal, stood Madame Neferuptah. I had not laid eyes on the artifacts until now. At first glance, there was little to remark. The stone was as Lord Silverpin had described it, dull black with equally dull red striations. However, as I examined it, I became aware of its strange angles, so odd my eyes and mind could not reconcile them, but neither could I tear my eyes away. Madame Neferuptah grasped my arm and pulled me back.

"Do not stand so close and do not look so deeply. It is not safe."

I turned my attention to the papyrus, dull beige in color with ragged edges and every inch of its surface covered with strange symbols. As I leaned in to examine the symbols, I drew back in disgust as the artifact appeared not to be papyrus paper but some kind of skin. I quickly turned away and joined Holmes who was conversing with Madame Neferuptah.

"Good luck to you, Madame," said he, and then, "Come, Watson. It is time."

Holmes and I returned to the ceremonial room and concealed ourselves in the shadows behind a large, painted screen. My nerves were on edge. I knew that somewhere in the rooms above, Inspector Crowe and his men were concealed. They had been smuggled in by Jim Gladney the day before, hidden in crates that appeared to contain garden statuary and farming implements. Jessup, stationed in the Great Hall, awaited the arrival of our adversary, ready to escort him into our trap. The Silverpins waited in a storage area adjacent to the ceremonial room. All was silent, save the soft hiss of the gas jets and Holmes's hushed breaths. The minutes crawled by and though I struggled to remain alert, my mind wandered, and my head nodded. More than once Holmes pinched me. I longed for something to break the monotony, a cigarette, a sip of sherry, a book. But Holmes had insisted on complete stillness and focus.

We had been crouching behind the screen for some time, and my weak leg threatened to cramp. I risked debilitating pain and immobility if I did not tend to it. I stretched carefully and did my best to alleviate the discomfort by massaging the muscles. While I was thus engaged, Holmes gripped my arm. A figure had entered the room. At first, all I could see was a long, undulating shadow, but then the shadow grew shorter as the being to which it belonged drew closer. Holmes held a finger to his lips, and we pressed ourselves deeper into the darkness.

As we watched, a creature of unhealthy pallor wrapped in a long cloak of some dark material emerged, a shadow from a shadow. So, this was the notorious Professor Emm. I can't say what I was expecting, but it was not this seemingly ordinary everyman who stood peering about like a myopic schoolmaster. He was tall and rail thin, with a high forehead, a beaky nose, and protruding eyes. His thinning hair was shot through with gray. His rounded shoulders gave him a stooping appearance. How had he gotten past the butler? If he had done Jessup some mischief, why had Inspector Crowe's men not intervened? It seemed Holmes's plan had already gone awry. I understood that we would have to take the villain on our own, which now, based on his appearance, did not seem such a daunting prospect. I had little doubt that between the five of us we could easily take Emm into custody.

As I surveyed the distance between Holmes, myself, and our visitor and weighed the possibilities of how best to overcome our quarry, a strong, sweet, evocative scent filled my nostrils. I sought its source and as I did so, I recognized the elusive fragrance of Lady Vivienne's perfume. First tendrils and then clouds of the stuff began to fill the room. Then, from out of the fog of incense, Lord Silverpin and Lady Vivienne, dressed as a pharaoh and his God-Wife, emerged. Lady Vivienne's form-fitting garment of sheer white linen left little to one's imagination. Lord Silverpin wore a short, pleated linen kilt. Bare-chested, his black hair fell to his waist, contained by the golden cobra circlet on the blue war crown upon his head.

Their eyes were rimmed with kohl. They wore elaborate pectorals of gold and semi-precious stones and golden sandals. They were sublime. They could have stepped from one of the paintings on the temple walls. Yet I could not imagine why they were dressed in such a way or their purpose in this increasingly strange scenario.

"What are they playing at?" I whispered.

Holmes held a finger to his lips. "We must trust them," he whispered in return, "if we are to win this war."

Emm turned toward us. His gaze lingered on our location long enough for me to imagine we had been discovered. But then, our visitor's contemptuous gaze returned to the Silverpins.

"What foolishness is this?" he rasped.

"The descendants of Amenhotep IV oppose you. See how your story is writ," said Lord Silverpin, pointing to one of the wall paintings.

Emm turned to stare at the painting and my gaze, too, followed the young Lord's finger. I had taken no particular notice of the painting that now held my attention. There in plain sight I saw a depiction of a pharaoh in a blue war crown portrayed as a giant. This giant leaned over the body of another much smaller pharaoh who knelt with bowed head and arms raised in supplication. In his raised hand, the giant brandished a serpent rod with arms of light emanating from a sun-disk held in the serpent's jaws, poised to strike a fatal blow to his adversary's head.

Emm uttered a sound of disgust. "I care nothing for your fairy tales. You are in possession of a stone and a papyrus that your father stole from me, and I will have them back."

Lord Silverpin and Lady Vivienne clasped hands and moved directly into Emm's path. Together they fixed their eyes upon him with an intense, unwavering gaze, and each lifted an arm with palm out-turned against him.

"Stay," Lord Silverpin said through clenched teeth. "You shall not pass."

Emm uttered a sound that I can only describe as an angry hiss as he swatted at the air surrounding his head as if batting away a swarm of pestering flies. His malevolent gaze seemed to strike the Silverpins with physical force. Their concentration broken, they staggered and fell back.

"Out of my way!" Emm snarled as he advanced on our clients.

It was a perfect distraction. With Emm's attention entirely upon Lord Silverpin and Lady Vivienne, Holmes tapped my arm and nodded. We rushed from our hiding place. I should say Holmes rushed. My leg was stiff and there was nothing I could do but limp after him. However, I had my revolver out and trained on Emm. Holmes strode over to him, manacles at the ready. He had his hand on our quarry's wrist when Emm turned abruptly and struck Holmes a powerful blow to the chest that sent him sprawling across the floor. As Holmes struggled to his feet, Emm moved to strike another blow. I aimed and fired. I am a crack shot and knew my aim to be true, but Emm kept moving as if unscathed. I'd seen men in battle spurred on by adrenaline keep fighting after sustaining multiple wounds. From outside the Temple came a cacophony of voices and within moments we were set upon by no less than six ruffians wielding cudgels and handguns. Holmes loosed an ear-splitting whistle, a pre-arranged signal that would summon Inspector Crowe and his men.

One of the thugs took aim at me. I dove for cover. A quick glance showed me Holmes, swordstick in hand, grappling with two other brutes who were intent upon his destruction. A bullet whistled past my ear, and I quickly turned my attention back to my own troubles. I barely had time to fire before three ruffians threw themselves upon me. I was pummeled viciously. My revolver, fallen from my hand, had been kicked away. With my arms pinioned to my sides, I could do nothing but strike out with my legs with as much force as I could muster. I took a nauseating blow to the stomach, and then I heard shouts and the pounding of boots. I rejoiced for the Inspector's assistance could not come soon enough. My attackers let me fall, distracted by the policemen who had burst into the room.

This brief respite allowed me to catch my breath and reclaim my weapon. My next thoughts were for Holmes and the Silverpins. The melee still raged around me, but Emm's men, now outnumbered by police constables, were losing ground to a superior force. I caught sight of Holmes just as he delivered a savage blow to the skull of an attacker, but the effort caused him to stagger and fall back against a wall.

A moment later, I understood why. Holmes clutched his side and I saw blood trickle between his fingers. The fighting had subsided. Emm's men lay sprawled upon the floor. I hurried to my friend, picking my way through the bodies.

Holmes, still supporting himself against the wall, looked precariously close to collapsing. I put my arm around him, supporting him as best I could. As I reached for his coat, he brushed my hand away.

"It is nothing, Watson, a flesh wound."

My hand came away stained with blood that had seeped through the fabric of his coat. "It is hardly that," I said. "I must get you upstairs where I can tend this wound properly. If there is a bullet in you, I will need to extract it."

Inspector Crowe appeared before us. "What a pack of devils," he said rubbing his jaw and flexing his fingers. "But we have the better of them." He made a quick appraisal of Holmes's condition then held out an arm to my friend.

"I'll give you a hand with him, Doctor."

Holmes gripped my arm fiercely. "No," he cried. You must find Emm and the Silverpins. The battle is not yet won."

He had barely spoken these words when a gunshot blast assaulted our ears followed by a terrible scream from the adjacent chamber. For a moment, as the acrid odor of gunpowder mixed with the incense, Holmes, Crowe, and I stood transfixed, frozen by that agonizing cry. I immediately thought of Madame Neferuptah alone in the inner sanctum protecting the artifacts. It is then we saw Emm, gun in hand, backing away from that very room pursued by Madame Neferuptah. She walked with difficulty, limping and laboring for breath. A trail of blood lay in her wake. Emm had his weapon trained upon her heart and yet she continued to advance. In her hand was the serpent rod — the same rod as in the wall painting! I saw the Silverpins, disheveled and bloodied, their faces contorted in horror, rushing toward her in an effort to support her, and I followed.

Suddenly, eyes blazing with rage, Emm turned on me, his face twisted with malevolent hatred. I staggered as if struck a physical blow. I was staring into the eyes of a demon. His lips moved and it seemed to me that he spoke silently, yet I could hear every word resonating in my mind, overwhelming my will.

Red. Javelin. Turnkey. Carriage. Carnelian. Bottle. Kill Sherlock Holmes.

I turned, aimed my service revolver, and fired. Holmes staggered and fell. In an instant, I was myself again, and the import of what I had done filled me with horror. I looked around wildly. Who had seen what I had done? The Silverpins turned their eyes upon me and suddenly the revolver seared my hand and grew hotter still until I flung it away with a cry, my palm and fingers red and blistered. My only thought now was to get to my friend, to save him, to heal him, to undo this foul and ultimate act of betrayal which I had committed.

Emm turned again to Madame Neferuptah. Supported by her son, she remained standing, shoulders hunched, knees sagging. Emm's venomous gaze bore down on her, and she crumpled, her body convulsing as her features contorted into a grimace of agony. She cried out as she thrust the serpent rod into Lord Silverpin's hands. He took it from her. She made no other sound but dropped motionless upon the floor bleeding to death before our eyes. Lord Silverpin fell to his knees and gathered her into his arms. Lady Vivienne, standing guard over her brother and mother, did not take her eyes from their mother's assailant. Emm, with look of derision, strode past them toward the inner sanctum.

"No!" cried Lady Vivienne as she leapt at him. Emm brushed her aside. She fell, cursing him, then her head struck the floor, and she moved no more.

"Watson!" Holmes shouted.

I turned to see my friend on his feet. Having seen him fall, I could not fathom where his strength came from. My mind rejected what was before my eyes, but my heart rejoiced at the sight of him. I moved to his side as he stepped between Emm and the entrance to the inner sanctum. At the sight of Holmes alive and adversarial, an utterance came from Emm that I can only describe as an ominous, predatory growl. As he glowered at us, a strange miasma gathered around his body. It began as an aura of black striated light that expanded and contracted. With each pulsation, his appearance altered. At first, his form and features blurred, and then slowly coalesced into a swarthy skinned being in pharaoh's garb, black eyes blazing from his cruel, imperious face. Now an entirely different entity stood before us. One that made my blood run cold for I recognized the creature from the description given by William Blough at the Egyptian Hall. The devil that stood before us was none other than the Black Pharaoh. Revulsion, then fear welled up in my breast. My skin crawled and a cold sweat trickled down my back. The assault upon my senses was excruciating, yet I could not turn my eyes away.

Behind this monstrosity, Lord Silverpin struggled to regain his feet. The look upon his face was dreadful, as if a great force pressed upon him and every inch claimed caused him great pain. Inspector Crowe rushed to his aid, and with his assistance, Lord Silverpin was able to rise. He gripped the serpent rod and lurched forward, one arduous step after another, until he reached us, whereupon he turned and thrust the serpent rod into the face of the monster. Our adversary responded with a roar of rage, and suddenly the air was alive with a black, buzzing wind that swarmed around us like a cloud of enraged bees. At the same time, I became aware of a growing pressure in my head as a powerful unease overtook my mind. As I struggled against this burgeoning anxiety, my limbs and body were wracked with pain as my muscles cramped violently. I fell to the floor howling. Around me, I heard others screaming. Fear gripped me, fear that quickly turned to abject terror as visions of unimaginable horrors swept through my mind — my withered limbs disintegrating and re-growing into slimy, sucker-studded tentacles; the bodies of my friends torn apart and transformed into grotesque, featureless lumps of flesh; the world crushed, burned black, and smoking beneath an alien sky. I was barely aware of what went on around me, but in brief flashes, I saw Lord Silverpin lashed mercilessly by that black wind, yet he remained on his feet, the serpent rod gripped tightly in his hand. I could see arms of light emanating from the sun in the serpent's mouth and where those rays struck the Black Pharaoh, they burned him, and his skin blistered and smoked.

The pain I was experiencing was unbearable. If I did not lose consciousness from that alone, the terrifying visions that continued to assault my mind would surely do the job. I struggled to stay conscious, but my strength drained away with the effort. For a moment, the relentless horrors behind my eyes subsided. It was in those few moments that I saw the Egyptian gods advancing into the chamber—the painted statues from the corridor had come alive! They seemed to encounter an unseen barrier that slowed their approach, but then in unison they turned their heads toward the Black Pharaoh, and I felt a wave of powerful energy roll over me. This force opened the way for the animal-headed gods, and they soon formed a circle around the evil creature. They spoke no word, yet the room filled with sound, no longer the howl of the black wind but a high-pitched whine that seemed to me to be the color of gold. The Black Pharaoh grasped his head, his hands pressed tightly against his ears, but as the whine increased to a deafening pitch, it forced our adversary to his knees. Lord Silverpin stepped into the circle of gods and smote the Black Pharaoh's head with the serpent rod. A great explosion of light burst over us and that is the last that I remember until Holmes brought me back to my senses.

Where the Black Pharaoh had stood lay the body of Professor Emm. He was still, and the twisted position of his limbs caused me to believe the man was dead. As if reading my mind, Holmes assured me that Emm was still alive, and that we finally had the fiend in custody. Holmes approached the prone figure and snapped the manacles around his wrists. He removed his cravat and tied it around Emm's mouth, gagging him. He then pulled a hood, not unlike the hood the hangman had placed upon Staunton, from his coat and covered Emm's head.

"Do not remove the hood or the gag until you have him securely locked in a cell. Two men must attend him at all times.

He must never be alone with anyone," Holmes instructed the constables as they dragged the prisoner away.

Holmes's eyes darted from one area of the ceremonial room to another.

"Where is Inspector Crowe?" he asked.

The Inspector had been there a moment ago, speaking with the Silverpins and the Osirans, but now he was nowhere to be seen.

"Hurry, Watson!" Holmes called out as he made for the inner sanctum.

Still addled from the mental assault, I stumbled after him. When I caught up with him, he stood by the pedestal where the stone and the papyrus had been secured. The gaslights still blazed, but the stone and the papyrus were gone.

"Good lord, "I cried. "Where can they be?"

"With Crowe," said Holmes, his voice tight with anger. "My brother's representative has been with us all along and has departed with the artifacts."

"Crowe?"

Holmes nodded.

"Let us get after him!" I cried.

Holmes put a restraining hand on my arm. "We will not find him. He was Mycroft's fail-safe against me."

"What?"

"He rightly deduced that I would not blindly turn over the artifacts to the government."

Lord Silverpin, Lady Vivienne, and the host of Osirans crowded into the inner sanctum. Lord Silverpin and Lady Vivienne stared in shock at the empty pedestal. The Osirans erupted in a cacophony of voices.

"Who?" Lord Silverpin demanded.

"Inspector Crowe acting for my brother, if I am not mistaken," said Holmes.

"You observed him?"

"No. However, he is nowhere to be found."

As we made our way back to the Temple's ceremonial room, we all goggled at the sight of Inspector Aloysius Crowe and two of his men standing in the middle of the chamber.

"I'm glad to see you are all in one piece," said he. "That was quite a bangarang."

I looked at Holmes.

Crowe was finally taking in our expressions.

"What has happened?" he asked.

"Someone has taken the artifacts," I said.

The shock that registered on his features in my opinion could not be feigned, except perhaps by the most skilled of thespians, and I did not think him that.

"Constables!" the Inspector shouted. "Seal the house. Let no one leave."

Chapter Twenty-Six

A few days later, home and safe, Holmes and I relaxed by the fire, basking in its warmth, and enjoying some of Mrs. Hudson's excellent cocoa. A soft, purple twilight had begun to settle over Baker Street as we listened to the distant tintinnabulation of church bells ringing vespers. An evening breeze whispered at our windows carrying with it the last cries of the street vendors and newsboys now wending their way home. The house itself was still, save for the occasional faint sounds of our landlady going about her business downstairs. We were awaiting the arrival of Inspector Crowe. He had sent a telegram stating he had news related to the Silverpin case.

"Hark," said Holmes as the bell clanged in the lower hall. "He is here already. What news can he have that has brought him with such speed?"

Inspector Crowe entered our sitting room in disarray, his clothing rumpled, his hair disheveled, and his collar sprung.

"Mr. Holmes, Dr. Watson, I have been up all night and day," said he. "You will hardly believe what I am going to tell you. I can barely credit it myself."

Holmes and I both snapped to attention at his unorthodox appearance and considerable agitation.

"What the devil is it, man?" Holmes said. "Come, out with it."

Inspector Crowe dropped into a chair and gulped the brandy I offered him. He looked first at Holmes, then at me, with an intense yet distracted gaze. He ran a hand through his hair and made an effort to collect himself before beginning his tale.

"Yesterday, I received an anonymous message informing me of the locations of two bodies. The first body we recovered in an untenanted house. In fact, Doctor, it was the very same house in which you were held captive. From documents found on the body and his calling cards, we identified the deceased as Professor J. Ambrose Emm."

"What?" I cried. "Emm is …"

Holmes, now sitting rigidly upright in his chair, forestalled me with an impatient wave of his hand.

"The police surgeon says he's been dead a week or more. Well before the events at Highmount House."

"How is that possible?" I cried. "If not Emm, then who is the man in your cells?"

"I have no idea," said Crowe. "And we are not likely to find out, for he is no longer in our cells. This morning when the guards delivered his breakfast, he was gone, vanished right from under our noses and, as yet no clue how."

"Well, well, I am not surprised," said Holmes. Rising from his deep armchair, he moved to the window and gazed down into the street. "I did warn you. Moriarty has agents everywhere. You mentioned a second body."

"Yes," said Crowe. "We found the second floating in the Thames. It was that of Dr. Scarabus. Inspector Lestrade identified him. They'd had a past encounter, it seems."

"Eliminating the competition," Holmes murmured.

'What's that you say, Mr. Holmes?" Crowe asked.

"Moriarty," said he. "He is eliminating the competition."

"Holmes, are you saying you believe it was Professor Moriarty whom we encountered in the Temple?" I asked.

"There is no doubt in my mind."

"But how can that be?" I cried "Surely, the Silverpins knew Professor Emm by sight."

Holmes retrieved a plug of tobacco from the Persian slipper on the mantle, took up his pipe, and returned to his chair. "The Silverpins encountered Emm only twice before they abandoned the London temple, and then not intimately, as his reputation caused them to avoid him. That the Silverpins did not recognize an impostor in the heat of the moment teaches us something of inestimable value, Watson."

"Emm and Moriarty are of a similar appearance," I said.

"Just so" declared Holmes. "We now have an idea of Moriarty's true appearance."

Inspector Crowe had risen from his chair and was now pacing the room, shaking his head and gesticulating with his hands. "But neither this Moriarty nor any of his men reached that inner chamber. They could not have carried away the artifacts."

"The scene was chaos," said Holmes. "And for some period, we were all insensible. I remind you, Inspector, of the question we must ask."

"What is that?" asked Inspector Crowe.

"If he did not enter through the house, how did Moriarty gain access to the Temple? Jessup was at the main door and the other doors were fastened tight and had guards on them."

"I have asked myself that question, Mr. Holmes. Surely, someone inside the house must be complicit. Jessup might have been mesmerized, but my men …"

A sudden realization struck me. "The tunnel," I cried.

"What is this?" demanded Inspector Crowe. "What tunnel?"

"Did I not mention the tunnel, Inspector?" said Holmes. "I do beg your pardon. I anticipated his entering that way. That is why there was no guard upon it. That would have given up the game."

Inspector Crowe turned incredulous eyes upon Holmes. "But how could you have known?"

Holmes, puffing on his pipe and looking rather pleased with himself, replied: "I developed a theory, rather late in the investigation, unfortunately, that Emm and Moriarty were working together from the beginning. It is the only theory that accommodates all the facts. However, at some point in their association, they had a falling out. I suspect that it occurred because Emm became obsessed with revenge and that interfered with Moriarty's designs. Or, Moriarty may have discovered that Emm intended to double-cross him, which I believe to be the case. If so, Emm was a fool. As you can clearly see that poor decision led to his death."

For a while, we three sat thoughtfully staring into the flames. After a long silence, Holmes the first to speak. "And it is because of the tunnel that I cannot be certain that all of Moriarty's men were accounted for. Can you?" Holmes asked Inspector Crowe.

Crowe hesitated for a moment. I believe the man dearly wanted to answer in the affirmative, but at last he said "No, I cannot."

He glanced at Holmes, but then his eyes lingered on me. "I cannot quite wrap my mind around all that has happened."

"Neither can I," I replied.

"It's all well and good to talk of hypnosis, but what I experienced …" he trailed off.

"Was more than can be explained in such terms," I offered.

"Exactly," he said. "How do you explain it, Mr. Holmes?"

"I am not susceptible to hypnosis, and I suspect you are not either, Inspector," said Holmes. "But we are all susceptible to drugs. Do you recall the clouds of incense that enveloped us when the Silverpins appeared?"

Inspector Crowe and I both nodded.

"We were all drugged," said Holmes. "The incense contained an ingredient that enhances the mind's abilities for mental projection and telepathic communication for wont of better terms. The Osirans use these methods to enhance their practice of theurgy, an act combining evocation and henosis, in order to achieve unity with a god, demon, or power outside of human awareness."

"We all hallucinated the same thing, didn't we? Experienced the same physical and mental assault? How is that possible?" Crowe demanded.

"I cannot answer that with authority at the moment, Inspector," Holmes said with a decided edge to his voice. "But I can say, we were surely primed for it. I beg you to recall where we were — an Egyptian temple. Recall the appearance of the Silverpins. Recall the painting on the wall that foretold the battle and its outcome and recall the Osirans dressed as the animal-headed gods we took for statues in the corridor. It was all there, waiting for our minds to make use of it."

Inspector Crowe shook his head and turned a questioning eye on my friend. "None of this helps us in recovering the artifacts. Everyone was searched, including the body of the woman, Neferuptah. Tell me where on Lord Silverpin or his sister the things could have been hidden. They were all but naked. Every Osiran was searched by you, Mr. Holmes. My men and I all submitted to a search. You tell me, Mr. Holmes where are the artifacts? It would seem they disappeared into thin air!"

"It is possible they are still at Highmount House."

"Rubbish! You cannot be serious? We have searched every inch of it!"

"I very much doubt that," said Holmes. "Highmount House has upwards of two hundred rooms not to mention a multitude of secret nooks and crannies which I wager have not yet been discovered."

"What are we to do then?"

"Nothing."

"Holmes!" I cried.

Inspector Crowe's eyes narrowed. "Nothing? After all that has transpired?"

"I have accomplished what I was employed to do," said Holmes. "I found my clients' father. They now know what fate befell him. His killer is dead. That at least is some justice. The artifacts are of no concern to me or to this case other than their usefulness in luring Moriarty into a trap. For that matter they are no concern of yours either, Inspector, beyond your obligation to secure them and turn them over to my brother if I failed to oblige him."

A fleeting smile passed over the inspector's lips.

Holmes barked a laugh. "I have known for some time that you were one of Mycroft's men. You are far too canny to be one of the Scotland Yarders."

"I'll take that as a compliment, Mr. Holmes."

"You may do so," replied Holmes. "Do give my regards to my brother. I hope our paths will cross again, preferably unencumbered by any governmental string pulling."

"I am not a government lackey, Mr. Holmes."

"I thought not. Queen's Secret Service, is it?"

"It is. Special Unit BEACON."

"Well, well," said Holmes. "Thank you for that bit of information. That clears up a few loose ends quite nicely. Though I am surprised you mention it."

Crowe chuckled. "I mention it because I know you will not repeat it."

Holmes's eyes twinkled and he tapped the side of his nose with a forefinger. "Be assured. I shan't repeat it."

Crowe nodded. "Until we meet again, Mr. Holmes, Doctor Watson," said he as he passed out of our sitting room, onto the landing, and down the stairs.

My mind was in a whirl. "What is BEACON?" I asked, not sure at all that I wanted to know.

"Ah," said Holmes. "BEACON stands for the British Empire's Advisory Council on Objects Non-Terrestrial."

"Oh," I said. "I wasn't aware such an agency existed."

"Few are. Speaking of beacons," he continued. "You might be interested to know that the scarabs were not left after the murders as the police believe. They were left prior to the murders to act as beacons to draw the killer to his victims."

"Left by whom?"

"They were most likely left by Emm himself or a confederate. As to how they work, I can only surmise from my own experience, of which you are already aware."

The evening was well-advanced, and Mrs. Hudson had been up with our supper before I plucked up the courage to speak with my friend about the heavy burden that encumbered my mind and soul. Holmes had not mentioned my attempt to kill him except to acknowledge that, like Staunton, I had fallen victim to the villain hypnotist. Still, I was wracked with guilt.

"Holmes," I said. "Can you forgive me for trying to kill you?"

My friend reached out and patted my arm. "Dear old friend do not trouble yourself. After your abduction and seeming amnesia, I foresaw such a scenario and when you insisted on coming with me, I loaded your gun and ammunition box with blanks."

"Good heavens," I said. "That never occurred to me."

Holmes chuckled. "Apparently, it did not occur to Moriarty, either."

While I was grateful for my friend's absolution, my mind remained troubled.

"I am afraid that I might be forced to try to kill you again and it seems my will is so weak, I cannot prevent it."

Holmes's expression was pensive as he folded his napkin and pushed away his plate.

"There is that possibility, of course. But I am told that the hypnotist's influence diminishes over time. I have spoken to Dr. Hyslop at Bethlehem Hospital on your behalf. He is eager to assist you and hopefully provide a bulwark against recidivism."

"I'm grateful," I said, my heart somehow heavier than before. I changed the subject before anymore could be said.

"If Moriarty expected us to be at Highmount, why did we pretend to leave?"

"So, it would appear that we were carrying out what Moriarty saw as our foolish plan. If we had not, that would have appeared suspicious."

"But how could you know that Moriarty would appear at a pre-arranged time?"

"Because, Watson, in his arrogance, he believed himself unbeatable. Why should he waste the effort of storming the castle when we were willing to open the door for him?"

"But surely, he did not expect us to be unarmed."

"Of course not, but neither did he expect to lose to the likes of us, not with the power and resources he had at his disposal. We did little more than create a much-needed distraction, while the Silverpins and the Osirans carried the day."

Holmes excused himself from the table and went to his bed chamber. When he returned, he was wearing his purple dressing gown, a sure sign of his good humor. He poured two glasses of port, handed one to me, and offered a toast to our victory. We raised our glasses, drank deeply, and then settled into our armchairs, he to peruse his crime indexes and I to read my new book by Wilkie Collins, *The Legacy of Cain*. However, try as I might, and despite my keen interest in the text, I could not keep my attention on my book, for a lingering question niggled at my mind.

"Holmes, if you are right about the artifacts, will not Moriarty continue to seek them?"

"Oh, undoubtedly, Watson. Undoubtedly."

"Do you truly believe the artifacts are with the Silverpins? Surely there are other possibilities."

"There are always possibilities, Watson. Why," said he with a wink of his eye, "anyone might have them."

THE END

ACKNOWLEDGEMENTS

I am tremendously grateful to all the people who helped me along on this book journey. First, my son, Justynn for encouragement and support. And, many thanks to Kristina Stanley, founder of Fictionary, and Ali Bumbarger and Lucy Cooke, certified Fictionary StoryCoach editors, for their brilliant structural edit of the manuscript. A special thank you to my copy editor, Mary Davis, for her insights and attention to detail. My very sincere thanks to first readers Weldon Burge, Patrick Derrickson, Krystina Schuler, and J. Patrick Conlon for their time, suggestions, and encouragement. Big thanks to Steve Emecz and all the staff at MX Publishing for undertaking the publication of this book. And last, but hardly least, thank you to the Delaware writing community and the many friends who cheered me on at every milestone.

ABOUT THE AUTHOR

JM Reinbold is an award-winning author and editor. A fan of Sherlock Holmes from an early age, Sherlock Holmes and the Adventure of the Black Pharaoh is her first Holmes novel. It was a great deal of fun to write, and another Holmes adventure is in the works. She is also the author of Missing, book one of the DCI Rylan Crowe Mysteries, and a collection of haiku poetry A Slow Gathering of Light. Her short stories, haiku poetry, and articles appear in anthologies, journals, and magazines in print and online, and in other media. She is a member of Mystery Writers of America.

You can visit her at www.jmreinbold.com